S0-EDQ-890

GORDON R. DICKSON

SF

ace books

A Division of Charter Communications Inc.
A GROSSET & DUNLAP COMPANY

51 Madison Avenue
New York, New York 10010

ON THE RUN

Copyright © 1956 by A. A. Wyn, Inc.
Originally published as MANKIND ON THE RUN

An ACE Book

Cover art by Roger Stine

This Ace printing: November 1979

2 4 6 8 0 9 7 5 3
Manufactured in the United States of America

ON THE RUN

CHAPTER ONE

THE south-bound rocket, intercontinental, out of Acapulco, Mexico, for Tierra del Fuego at the tip of South America, flamed skyward east of the city, briefly ripping apart the soft tropical night with sound and fury. Its glare dwindled and vanished, leaving only the little firefly lights of small flyers, dropping down into the shallow bay before the Hotel Belmonte. On the terrace of the hotel's open-air dining area, cut from the rocky cliffs and facing the ocean, Kil Bruner turned from the noise of the departing rocket to see his wife, Ellen, dabbing furtively at her eyes.

"You're crying?" he said. "What is it?"

Ellen brushed hastily at her eyes with shaky fingers.

"Don't—I'm not crying," she answered. "I'm just happy, that's all. Happy on our anniversary." She turned her head away. "Don't look at me,

1

please, Kil. Look over on the terrace. Is the diver coming yet?"

Kil scowled blackly, and slowly removed his gaze to the terrace, which extended to the mouth of the gorge on which the hotel was built. He was not by nature a biddable young man. His first articulate word, according to his mother, had been no. "That boy would say no," she was in the habit of saying, "if—" and there words always failed her. She had died in the same London-Capetown rocket crash that had killed his father, but her tall, rebellious son had continued to live according to her pronouncement with the imagination-provoking gap at the end.

In the case of Ellen, however, it was a little different.

So he did look over the terrace, past the rocky gorge into the small bay where the flyers nestled close on the water in parked ranks, like sleepy water fowl under the moon. Beyond them, the silver-dark ocean spread wide to the horizon; and far out, a whale blew, its plume of exhausted breath going up like a tiny, white finger, frosty for a second in the moonlight before it disappeared.

Closer in, the terrace murmured darkly with shadowy forms, lounging and moving about. To the right, spotlighted by the pure bottled daylight of sunbeam lamps from the top of the old hotel, the dining area's main floor murmured brightly. Men in tunics and kilts, or trousers clipped tight at the ankle, talked and laughed with women in slacks, shorts, or skirts of all lengths. Here and there, the Key on someone's wrist gleamed even among the gleaming colors of the crowd. And in the gorge below, the water, mounting the tide, crashed and foamed high against the rocky walls. The orchestra played dance music.

"Kil—" it was Ellen's voice. "You can look back now."

He turned again to her. Her face, like some small flower, seemed almost freshened by the brief summer shower of her tears. Out of the brightness of the sunbeams illuminating the dance-floor, back in the shadow of moonlight where they sat, her face was beautiful, small and perfect, oval and delicate, blue eyes under soft blonde hair.

"Don't look like that, Kil," she said. "It's nothing. Really it isn't." She put out a hand to touch his arm. "Happy fifth anniversary, sweetheart. I love you."

"Well," he said gruffly. "I love you."

She looked at him, sadly affectionate. Her fingers went up to rub gently away at the frown on his forehead.

"Dark and angry man," she said.

He made an effort to smooth his expression out. In the mirror of her eyes he saw himself as something different. He was tall and lean, angular of face, black-browed, and scowling with habitual impatience. "I'm ugly," he had told her once, five years ago, with harshness. "But it's a beautiful ugliness," she had answered. Seeing himself reflected now in the magic crystal of her love, he almost believed it.

"What was it?" he insisted.

"Nothing . . . nothing . . ." she repeated; but her eyes seemed to glisten again for a second, in the moonlight. "I'm just sad about leaving, that's all."

Automatically, reflexively, he glanced at the Key on her wrist and, from it, to the Key on his own. Above the Class A designation on the dials, and below the code numbers, the calchronometer of each showed twenty-seven hours remaining of the six months permitted them in one location.

"We've had our period here," he said.

"I know." But her face was still unhappy.

"Nobody gets more than that," he said. "Why does it always bother you so much, Ellen?"

"Because I want a home!" she burst out suddenly. "Because I want to settle down—oh, darling, don't ask me about it tonight. Look, Kil. Look, there's the diving boy coming now."

His attention forced away, Kil looked over toward the terrace, following the direction of her pointing finger. The diving boy, or rather, his simulacrum—the plastoid automaton imitation of a diving boy who once had been, back before Acapulco and everyplace else were more than just names on a map—was coming down the steps. Brown and compact, in trunks, and very lifelike, it descended to the lowest level of the terrace, climbed over the stone balustrade, and dived from view. A second later, its head popped up through the foamy water in the mouth of the gorge and it swam across to begin its climb up the face of the cliff opposite.

"Ellen," Kil spoke to her profile, "there's been something on your mind lately—these past few weeks. What is it? Something about this next job? I don't have to take it, you know. If you don't want to go to Geneva, just say so. They need engineers everywhere; you know that. Just say where you'd like to go."

"Kil!" She reached blindly for his hand without turning her head. "It's not that. It's nothing, really."

"Then why won't you tell me about it? If it's nothing, you ought to be able to tell me what it is. Why all this dodging around the question? You'd think I was an Unstab who couldn't be trusted to hear—"

"Kil, please!" whispered Ellen, tightly. "People are staring at us. Look at that policeman over there."

Startled, Kil turned his head and looked out over the little wilderness of adjoining tables. Twelve or fifteen feet away, his glance suddenly locked with that of a man sitting along at a small table and gazing in their direction. The man wore no local uniform, but the insignia of the World Police, a bloody hand grasping the naked blade of an unsheathed sword, was on the front of his white tunic. As Kil's eyes met his, he looked away. Kil turned back to Ellen.

"What of it?" he demanded. "I've got a right to know."

"Wait!" She squeezed his hand fiercely with her own. "Wait until the diving boy's through."

Tight-jawed and grudgingly, Kil sank back into his seat and let his gaze shift toward the gorge. The simulacrum had reached the top of the cliff now. The music of the orchestra stopped abruptly and a rolling of drums burst forth, shatteringly loud on the eardrums, echoing between the narrow walls of the gorge. The small, brown figure approached the edge of the cliff.

Kil stole a glance at Ellen. Her eyes were closed, her face tilted back a little and held still as if against some arrowing inner pain. She seemed to hold her breath. Watching, Kil felt the sudden explosion of instinctive alarm bells within him.

"Ellen!" he cried.

He started to reach out for her. And the world stopped.

It was no small stopping. Everything ceased: everything froze. On the top of the cliff, the diver, bright-lit from below by the red glare of a fire of paper that had been kindled in the gorge, checked suddenly, leaning out at an impossible angle over emptiness. The sea became rippled glass, with a whale spout hanging tiny, and half-finished on the horizon. In the dining area, people stood and sat like arrested marionettes. The drummer poised his sticks in mid-roll and all sound stopped.

Locked in stillness, like everything else, Kil strained to turn his head, to move in any way, but could not. And then, from somewhere among the shadows on the terrace, there was movement.

At first it was something half-seen out of the corner of Kil's paralyzed vision. And then, as it came closer, it resolved itself into a straightly upright old man, as tall as Kil, with wide-set eyes in a smooth face; an old man dressed simply in kilt and tunic. For a second this alone registered with Kil, who could not understand the reason for the basic feeling of *wrongness* with which the sight of the man struck him. Then it hit home. A difference that set this stranger off from all the four billions of other human beings that roamed the earth.

The old man wore no Key.

He came up to the table where Kil and Ellen sat.

"Now, Ellen," he said. It was a deep, tired voice, a voice weary with years.

Behind him, Kil heard the soft whisper of her skirt as Ellen rose. She came around the table slowly and stood looking down for a long moment into Kil's eyes.

"Ellen," repeated the old man. "Ellen. Come now."

There was no doubt about the tears in her eyes now. She bent swiftly and kissed Kil on his immobile lips. Then she turned; and the old man led her away, down into the shadowy, motionless crowd on the terrace, and out of sight.

For a little while there was nothing. And then, like a sigh sweeping in from the sea, life and motion came back to everything and everyone. The fire flickered again and a wave, poised high against the cliffs of the gorge, fell back with a crash of water. The drummer's sticks finished their rolls; the diver dropped.

He splashed into the water and a moment later reappeared, his head breaking the surface, small and sleekly dark in the firelight. Applause mounted. Couples moved out on the floor, and the orchestra began to play a dance tune in counterpoint.

And at his table, Kil, able once more to move and speak, but facing an empty chair and an untouched drink, sat like a stone.

Sat like a stone. . . .

CHAPTER TWO

". . . on good authority. News of the past six hours mirrors no increase in general stability, rather a slight falling off of sixteen thousandths of one per cent, according to the latest estimate of Files, published forty minutes ago by World Police Headquarters at Duluth, Lake Superior Region. This is a variation quite within normal limits and the Police are not unduly concerned.

"Around the globe, there has been a minor outbreak of colds in North Berlin and the area has been quarantined, although local health control groups expect to have the matter well in hand within twelve hours. Present residents of the area have been advised that if they will present their Keys at any transportation checkpoint, they will automatically be reset to allow them an extra twelve hours stay within the area. In Tokyo, a riot flared briefly in the Slum Area as one faction of Unstabs met in pitched battle with another. Local *authorities quickly restored order, but they have requested the World Police to investigate.*

"At Police Headquarters in Duluth, an official denial was issued today in answer to the rumor that Files has advised a tightening of residence limits of any single location. The rumor, as it reached this news office, predicted that residence limits for all Stabs, Classes A, B, and C, would be cut in half; and all Unstabs reduced uniformly to one week's time in any single area. 'Not only has Files not volunteered a recommendation for such a change,' said Hagar Kai, present six-month head of World Police today, 'but we have advanced the question on a hypothetical basis and Files has responded negatively.' The World Union of Astrophysicists is meeting in Buenos Aires today; and elsewhere in the world—"

The polite, indifferent murmuring of the news announcer, from the vision box recessed in the wall of the manager's office, crept forth to coil itself about the exhausted silence that had fallen among the three men. The local police chief sighed and shrugged.

"What can I say?" He was heavy-boned, immovable in appearance, but he spoke Basic with the swallowed consonants and slurred vowels of an Oriental. "You say something happened—"

"It did!" cried Kil. He thrust his wrist with the Key on it under the uniformed man's nose. "Read it! Do you think I'm having delusions? Do you think I'm psychotic? Unstab?"

"No, no. I can see. You're Class A," replied the chief, wearily.

"Then why won't you believe me?"

"Because it is a lie!" shouted the manager of the

hotel, excitedly. He was a slim, little, dark man and he literally pushed himself up on his toes with the violence of his argument. "I was there. Dozens of people were there. Nothing happened. Nothing stopped. I say so. Everyone else says so. If his wife left she must have just—" he threw both arms wide to the walls of the office —"walked off!"

Kil turned his head and looked at the small and noisy man and, inside him there was an urge to commit murder. The Police chief put a calming hand on his arm.

"Look," he said.

Reluctantly, Kil turned back to him.

"Look," said the Police chief, again. "You have to admit your story's fantastic. All right, maybe it happened. We're not savages who're going to yell impossible at the first strange word we hear. But you know I can't help you. I shift areas every six months, too. Violations of local ordinances— they're my job. You know whom to see."

He stopped and gazed steadily at Kil. Kil stared back.

"You mean *the* Police," he said.

"The World Police. Right." The chief paused, still staring earnestly at Kil. "They've got the organization. They've got Files."

Kil felt emptiness wash through him. He stood up.

"All right," he said harshly. "I will."

He turned and went out.

Outside, the first clear, bright light of tropical morning took him by surprise. The night, since Ellen had disappeared, had seemed endless; he was almost a little shocked to see the daylight now, as if the world was committing a callous indecency to go its way in ordinary fashion when his own small part of it had been so shattered and overthrown. Feeling cold and somewhat empty, he stepped forward onto the rollers and from the rollers onto the moving roadway. He let the great, free transportation system that had shaped his life since childhood, carry him down the hill and away.

At the Los Angeles-bound magnetic line, a long, slim, fifty-passenger craft floated in air within the large magnetic rings of its cradle. Ahead of it, the line of rings stretched along its route, up and over the edge of a mountainside, distance making them seem to close into a tube as they dwindled in perspective. As he stepped through the ship's entryway, Kil reached out automatically to present the face of his Key to the checkbox there. There was no sound from the Key but its calchronometer reading popped over to show a full six months before another move would be required.

The mag ship had been all but full of passengers when he came up and he had little more than taken his seat when the *fasten safety belts* sign lit up. The door sucked shut, the ship floated gently forward out of the cradle and began to pick up speed between the spaced rings. The ground alongside blurred and spun away. At a little under a thousand miles an hour, the mag ship streaked for Los Angeles, the thunder of torn air in its passage echoing among the mountains in its wake.

It was close to seven o'clock when Kil reached

Los Angeles. An intra-continental rocket was leaving for Duluth in the Lake Superior region at seven forty-five. Kil had some coffee and then boarded it. Forty minutes later, acceleration slammed him back in his seat, the earth fell away beneath him an enormous distance, then drifted slowly back again as the rocket glided down to Duluth. He stepped out at Duluth Terminal at three minutes after eleven, local time.

He had never been to the Lake Superior Region and World Police Headquarters before. The breeze of the lake was cool and brisk, although it was late May. To save time, he caught an aircab at the entrance, dialed dispatcher information and explained his problem.

"Complain Section Aj493," said the cab speaker. It took off, flitted for some fifteen minutes between tall buildings, was halted for beam-check at an entry point, and then allowed to continue, flying low and following a rigid route to a low, white building overlooking the lake itself.

"Complaint Section," announced the cab, landing before the entrance and opening its door. Kil read the meter, took a roll of credit units from his packet and tore off a strip of the soft metal tabs. The meter gulped them with a click and thanked him. He got out and went inside the building.

Within the front door, he found himself in what looked like a large, low-ceilinged auditorium, all broken up into small booths and compartments. The first row of these facing him, was nothing more than half-cubicles, like open visorphone booths, each one having a panel containing a speaker slot and microphone. As Kil stepped into the nearest one, and pressed his Key into the waiting cup, a little light went on at the top of the panel.

"State your complaint," said the speaker slot. "It will be electronically sorted and you will be directed to the proper human interviewer for detailed interview."

"My wife is missing," said Kil.

"Missing person," echoed the slot. The panel swung back, revealing a hallway with rows of numbered doors. "Go directly to the interviewer in room 243. Use your Key. Room 243 is the only door that will open to it."

Kil walked through. Behind him, the panel swung shut, to await the next complainant. He went down the hallway, reading the door numbers until he came to 243. It was a door like all those that he had been familiar with since childhood, perfectly blank except for the Key-sensitive cup in the center of it.

He lifted his Key and pressed it into the cup. The door swung noiselessly back before him and he stepped into a small room, where a uniformed young woman, blonde and attractive, sat behind a desk banked with coder keys. She smiled professionally at him.

"Sit down," she said, waving him to a single chair facing the desk. "My job's to take down the details of your complaint and find out what officer you ought to be assigned to for action. Name?"

"Bruner, Kil Alan," he answered.

"Occupation?"

"Engineer, Mnemonics."

"Stab?

"Class A."

"Let's see your Key." She leaned over and inspected it, reading off Kil's individual number, the number under which Kil was known to the computer memory of Files. Kil watched her tap it out on her coder keys. He had not thought of it until now, but suddenly he realized that her keys must connect directly with Files itself, and that his case would be passed on and decided by Files. And, abruptly, at the thought of this living, human problem of his and Ellen's, going for decision before this great electronic monster, used to it as he was in all aspects of his life, he felt a sudden panic and a shrinking.

But the questions continued.

"Last resident? Last job? Name of missing person? Stab rating of missing person? Her occupation? Last seen? Describe in detail . . ." The questions continued in the woman's low pitched, dispassionate voice, and her fingers danced remotely over the coder keys as if they were something as detached from the human equation as Files itself.

Finally, the questions and answers came to an end. The woman, whose name-tag read "Kay," pressed the decision button and sat back. On the flat desk screen before her, numbers began to click out, one by one, appearing at regular and emotionless intervals. When the screen was filled and the numbers had stopped, she sat reading them, for the first time showing a hint of puzzlement in her eyes. She looked curiously at Kil, then back at the screen and pushed a key down twice, two hard, quick jabs of her forefinger.

The numbers flicked off the screen and flicked back on, unchanged.

"What's wrong?" asked Kil. "There's no mistake, is there?"

"Files doesn't make mistakes," she said. But it was a mechanical answer and the look of puzzlement remained until, with a conscious effort, she cleared the expression from her face.

"You go from here to another office." She looked at Kil. "The man you'll talk to there will be a Mr. McElroy. I'll send a wand along to show you the route."

She pressed a stud on her desk, a narrow slot opened in the wall of the cubicle, and one of the guiding devices she had mentioned rolled out. It was nothing more than a slender antenna sprouting from a small box-like receiver mounted on a floton—not a wheel, but a sort of underinflated sausage-shaped bag which could manage to go almost anywhere, short of up the side of a vertical wall. Kay reached down and made a setting on the box.

"Follow the wand," she said. Kil rose, then turned back to thank her, but she was looking at him with such a strange, curious expression in her eyes that he turned away again without a word and followed the wand into the hallway, for the first time since Ellen had gone, disturbed by something beyond the immediate problem of finding her again.

The wand trundled ahead of him, leading him down the hallway, off a branching corridor to a disk elevator. It rolled onto the first descending disk to come level with the floor of the corridor. Kil stepped hurriedly on beside it, and they dropped down to the next level.

Emerging into a new hallway, the wand went

on, guiding him through a complicated route that ended eventually before a plain door, no different from many others they had passed. Kil faced his Key into the cup and the door opened to show a square, middle-sized room, whose only remarkable feature was a window opening on the lake, on a level less than a dozen feet above the surface of the water itself. This, a desk and a few chairs, broke up the monotony of the place.

The room was empty and Kil, his gaze drawn irresistably to the window, felt a sudden wild and powerful wave of feeling sweep through him, staggering him. The sight of the lake had at one sweep brought back his memory of the sea in the moment when Ellen had left him. He swayed, putting out a hand to the antenna of the wand, to steady himself, and at that second, the door of the room opened behind him and a man's voice spoke to him.

"Mr. Bruner?"

Kil took his hand from the wand and turned to confront a short, dark, wiry-looking man perhaps a dozen years older than himself, in grey kilt and tunic with a small oval framing the Police emblem on each piece of clothing. The man did not wait to hear Kil acknowledge himself, but walked around Kil with a springy, athletic stride, to seat himself behind the desk.

"Sit down," he said, waving Kil to a facing chair.

Kil sat.

"You're McElroy?" he asked.

"That's right. Now—" McElroy leaned forward, putting both elbows on the desk. His thin, dark features were intense. "Suppose you run through it once more for me. Just what happened when your wife left you?"

Kil told him. McElroy listened without interrupting, elbows on the desk, hands clasped, his head a little on one side and eyes noncommitally on Kil's face.

When Kil had finished, McElroy nodded, straightened up and put his slim hands flat on the desk.

"Yes," he said. He looked across at Kil with an expression in which curiosity and sympathy were somehow mixed. "You know," he said softly, "we can't help you."

Kil stared at him, stunned.

"Can't help me?" The words seemed to be perfectly nonsensical noises with no meaning whatsoever.

"No." McElroy still regarded him.

"But you know where she is! I mean—Files will know the next time she checks her key. And you—"

"Yes. We can get the information from Files." McElroy still spoke softly. "But we won't." He seemed to be walking on eggs, verbally tiptoeing around some delicate subject.

"It's that business of the stopping!" said Kil suddenly. He stared furiously at the other man. "You don't believe me."

"No. Yes," said McElroy. "I mean it could have been true for you. You could have been hypnoed."

"I'm a bad hypnotic subject!"

"Still—with drugs? No, that's not the trouble. The trouble is, it's not our job."

"Not your job! You're public servants. You're—"

"No!" said McElroy, with such hard, sudden violence in his voice that it checked Kil. There was a small second of silence, then the Policeman went on in quieter tones. "We're set up to keep the peace. That's our job. To be the strong right arm of Files. That's why they started us, a hundred and fourteen years ago." He raised his eyes, suddenly, burningly, to Kil. "What do you know about it? You're Class A."

"What's Class A got to do with it?" demanded Kil, his ready anger flaring up to matching heat. A thought occurred to him. "Aren't you?"

"Yes, but I *know!*" said McElroy. "I've been in this business since Files recommended me for training school at thirteen. You don't. No Class A does. They're the cream of the crop, with six full months before they have to move from one location to another. What if you were Class B and had to move every three months? What if you were Class C and had to move every month? What if you were Unstab?"

"What's that got to do with it, I say?" snapped Kil. "I'm not Unstab."

"No," said McElroy, settling back in his chair. "You're not Unstab. You live almost the way they did in the old days. You don't sneak glances at your Key every fifteen minutes to see how many hours—hours, not days, are left before you have to catch a rocket or a mag ship and move again. You don't lie awake nights hating the world, hating Files, hating us, hating everything until you end up dreaming, staring into darkness and dreaming, of somehow getting your hands on a CH bomb just so you can blow us and the rest of the world, and

even your own sick and tortured self to hell and
end the whole damn sorry mess!''

McElroy ended suddenly on a high note of violence. The silence after his words seemed to rock
and swirl like torn-up water.

"You sould like an Unstab yourself," said Kil,
looking steadily at him.

"I'm not. If I were I couldn't be in the Police, of
course." McElroy ran a hand wearily through his
hair. "I'm just trying to make you understand.
You Class A's live in a fool's paradise. Just because you've been able to adjust to the world, you
forget the other nine-tenths of humanity who
haven't. You forgot there ever was a Lucky
War—"

"I don't!" Kil cut sharply in on him. "I had it
pounded into me when I was young, just like
everybody else. I know about the seven hundred
million dead in just the first twenty-four hours;
and how it was just by the smallest chance the
cobalt fallout didn't finish off the whole race. I
know. What of it? What's that got to do with
Ellen?"

"Your wife left of her own free will."

Kil stared at him.

"What do you mean?"

"I mean," said McElroy, patiently, "that forget-
ting this idea about things stopping, as being unimportant one way or another, you've told us only
that your wife stood up and walked out on you. If
requested to do so, we'll interfere where crimes of
violence are concerned. In the case of unexplained disappearances we'll investigate because
these might have something to do with an attempt
to break the peace. Neither applies in your case. A

check on your wife would only be a violation of her privacy."

"But she didn't want to go! I tell you she was crying when she left me!"

"This old man—did he grab her, use any kind of physical force?"

"No, but—"

McElroy shrugged.

"You see," he said. "All she's done is leave you of her own free will. She's perfectly within her rights as an individual to do that. No, there's no grounds for us to interfere, to divert trained time and energy from our more important job of keeping the world from blowing up. I couldn't recommend a check on your wife, and I wouldn't if I could."

"Wait—" cried Kil, remembering suddenly. "The old man. He wasn't wearing a Key!"

McElroy sat for a second, looking across the table at him. The policeman's eyes had hardened. They were even a little contemptuous.

"That's impossible."

"I saw it!"

McElroy softened. He sighed.

"And you saw everything stop while nobody else did." He stood up and walked around the desk. "No. If you don't mind my offering some advice, register a divorce. If you don't hear from her in six months, it'll be final and you can put her out of your mind. If you don't hear from her in six months, you *should* put her out of your mind. This is all new and a shock to you; but this sort of thing happens a lot nowadays. One partner gets tired of the other—"

"No! She would have told me!" burst out Kil.

"We didn't have anyone but each other, don't you understand? My parents are dead, and she was raised by grandparents who died before I met her." He glared at McElroy. "Don't think I'm stopping just because you tell me to. I'll appeal this to Files."

"If you want. But," said McElroy, going toward the door, "you'll just get a reaffirmation of what I've told you. I'm just giving you Files' decision now. You see," he laid his hand on the inner knob of the door and pulled it open. "That's why you were referred to me. That's my job—turning people down."

And he went out. The wand rolled forward from its position in a corner of the room, up to Kil's chair, and stood waiting.

CHAPTER THREE

THE Policemen in charge of the gate passed Kil out with a nod, and he emerged into a little paved area occupied by some loungers and a rank of aircabs. Gratefully, he went across to the first of the waiting line of cabs, stepped through its door and literally fell into the seat. On the panel before him a red light glowed suddenly into life; and the mechanical voice asked:

"Destination?"

"Nearest Class A hotel," answered Kil.

The cab stirred, on the verge of rising; but before it could take off, a small hunchbacked man came darting out of the crowd around the gate and grabbed at the door handle. The cab's safety checks arrested it. It settled back on the ground.

"Chief!" yelled the little man.

Kil turned and looked into a narrow, pointed face under straight black hair, grimacing at him through the cab's window. He leaned over and pressed the button that slid the window aside.

"What?" he asked.

"Chief!" cried the small man. "Chief, you need a runny? I'm a good one for any need you got. Go anywhere; handle anything."

"No!" growled Kil, stabbing the button and sending the window back again. "Take off!" he ordered the cab.

The cab lit up its *passenger's responsibility*, unblocked its safety checks and rose skyward. Kil saw the pointed face draw away below him and the cries of "Chief! *Chief!*" dwindle in the distance. Kil leaned back against the cushions of the cab and closed his eyes.

Exhaustion chilled him like a clammy hand, a giant's hand enclosing, and the world swam about him.

Later, he hardly remembered getting out at the hotel and taking a room. Once he touched the bed, he sank into sleep like a man drowning in its dark waters. When he woke again, it was night. The automatics of the room had opaqued the window against the stars and the city lights; and the only illumination came from the faintest of glows in the ceiling corners, where the room's sunbeams maintained a night-light intensity. Kil sat up, thumbed the window to clear, and, dialing up a drink, sat, nursing it and staring out at the night-time city.

The streets and buildings stretching away up the shoreline of the lake shone with their own lights. Only off to his right, in an area close to the traffic terminal, did the lighting falter and give way to patches of dimness and shadow. This would be the Slums—Slums of the World, as they

were occasionally called—the area which, in any
city, normally housed the greater portion of the
Unstabs currently in residence there. The buildings in the area were not, of course, slums in the
old sense of the word. In construction and quality
they were in every way the equal of the hotel Kil
was in right at the moment (its class rating did not
refer to the quality of a hotel, but the Stab rating of
the majority of people using it). It was not the
physical environment of these areas that caused
them to be called Slums, but the mental. Full of
psychological misfits and outcasts and downright
criminals, their internal lawlessness winked at by
World Police and local authorities as well, the
Slums were a breeding place of vice and violence.
Away in the opposite direction, in brilliant contrast, the clearly defined area of the World Police
Headquarters was a blaze of light. It ran up the
shoreline of the lake until it was lost in the distance, the public, unofficial areas of the city clustered inland from it and following along the out-
skirts.

Kil finished his drink, pushed the glass
through the spring-lid of the bedside disposal,
and got up. As he dressed, the hard purpose
within him, melted temporarily by sleep, formed
itself icily once again. The World Police had let
him down. All right, there were private services.

He looked them up in the city directory and
took an aircab to the building that housed them.
The watch built into his Key told him that it was
already thirteen minutes after eleven, but this did
not disturb him. The services and business in all
large cities worked clear around the clock, or else

traded hours with other establishments in the same line, so that there was always someone on hand to handle whatever might come up. This had come about naturally where everything was, by necessity, more or less geared to the great worldwide transportation system, itself a twenty-four hour a day proposition.

The detective services occupied two floors of the building; but on the wall directory near the building's entrance, only a cluster of numbers on the upper of these two floors was lit up, signifying the fact that they were open for business. Kil went up in the disk elevator and tried them, one after another. Disappointingly, the first three had nothing but automation receptionists, adequate enough for taking down details and explaining services and rates, but not liable to provide the immediate action Kil wanted. The fourth door, however, into which he faced his Key, opened to reveal a thin, nervous, stooped man who bounced to his feet, and came hurrying around his desk to introduce himself as Cole Marsk, freelance operative.

Marsk seated himself and listened jerkily, but attentively, as Kil told his story. The detective was a man of small gestures; scratching his chin, twitching papers on his desk first out of, then back into, position before him. His face, however, lengthened; and he bit his lips as Kil finished.

"Ah," he said. "Ah. That's too bad. Yes—" he swung about to look out of the office window, the pivot of his chair giving a ridiculous little squeak in the silent office as he did so, and another as he turned back again. "Yes, that's too bad."

"How soon can you get going on it?" demanded Kil.

"Well—now" answered Marsk, not looking at him, "that's it. One of these missing person cases. Of course I'd like your account; but there's really nothing I can do."

"Nothing?" Kil stared at him. The detective fidgeted and squirmed under his gaze.

"Nothing. I'm sorry—" Marsk hurried ahead, almost tripping over his own words, "—cases like this. What you need, you see, is a large organization. I'm Class C, myself—oh, not that I'm ashamed of it, but I can't afford an organization. Some of the big outfits might take your job. But no, they wouldn't. Risky."

"What do you mean, risky?" exploded Kil.

"You know, it might involve them in a civil suit for infringement of privacy, in a case where the individual didn't want to be located."

"But that's senseless. She's my wife!"

"Yes. Still—" Mark coughed, and avoided Kil's eyes.

"You mean to sit there," growled Kil, "and tell me I can't hire detectives to find my own wife?"

"Well—not those with heavy investments in the business," said Marsk. "And those without assets like that can't afford the organization. I'm just one man, myself. That wouldn't do you much good. You've got to check a good large share of the big population centers simultaneously. Even then, it might take years, or your wife might never be found."

Kil slammed his hand down furiously on the

arm of his chair and, jumping to his feet, strode toward the door.

"Wait—wait—" cried the detective, running after him. "Wait a minute. Maybe I can help you some other way."

Kil checked and swung about.

"What way?"

"I could give you some advice—some directions." A small cunningness crept into the thin man's eyes. "Of course I'd have to charge for it."

Kil's hands twitched. He had a sudden, almost uncontrollable desire to pick the other man up and break him open in search of some solid answer. He controlled himself.

"All right," he said. "What is it?"

"One thousand; in advance."

"One thou—" Belatedly Kil came to a recognition of the sort of man he was dealing with.

"I'll give you a hundred," he said.

"Two hundred."

"All right, two hundred," said Kil, harshly. He watched as Marsk ran to the desk and punched a stud for a facsimile draft. Kil walked over and made it out for two hundred units. Marsk triumphantly punched the stud again, and the facsimile disappeared, flashed instantaneously to Central Banking, to be deducted from Kil's account.

"Now talk," said Kil.

"All right I will." Marsk's voice was defensive. "You don't think I was thinking of holding back anything? I may be Class C, but I'm still Stab. The truth is, not even the big agencies can help you. Oh, they might, but the odds are against it. Even the ones with agencies and operatives in most of the larger spots can't really cover all the transportation centers; and that's where you do your locating when you want to find somebody.''

"You charged me two hundred to tell me this?" Kil could feel the deep, slow kindling of his rage beginning to burn inside him.

"No, no—that's just part of it. I just wanted to let you know the agencies couldn't do it. But maybe there's some people who can—" Marsk broke off suddenly and his eyes roamed jerkily about the room.

"What is it?" demanded Kil.

"A looper—nothing—" murmured Marsk. His voice picked up strength again. "I was going to say—the Unstabs.''

"The Unstabs!"

"Yes—not so loud," Marsk rubbed his hands together and then dried the palms of them on his kilt with a soothing motion. "I'm Class C. I don't have anything to do with them. But you learn things in this business. You go see a man called the Ace King."

"The Ace King?" Kil stared at the detective. "Who's he?"

"I don't know who he'll be. It's a title, not a name. It'll depend on who's in town at the moment. He'll be either a King or a Crim, though."

Kil regarded him suspiciously.

"What is this, double talk?" He leaned forward. "Kings, and Crims?"

Marsk laughed high in his nose, a whinnying sound.

"That's the way they talk," he said. "They've got names for themselves, for the three classes. Kings for Class One—''

"What three classes?"

Marsk stared at him, uncertain whether to laugh or be astonished.

"You know—the three classes—just like our three Stab classes. You know about them?"

"How should I know?" said Kil, harshly. "I don't have anything to do with Unstabs."

"Class One, Two, and Three," Marsk said, still looking uncertainly at him. "Class One is on three week permit. They're top, like our Class A's— like you with six months. They call themselves Kings. Then there's Class Two, on two-week. They're middle, like our three month Class B's. Call themselves Crims. Then the last are one-weeks. Like our C's. They're called Potes."

"Why?"

"Why—?" Marsk floundered, at a loss.

"Why're they called—what they're called? How'd they get these names?"

"Why, King—I don't know. Because they're top, I suppose," said Marsk. "Oh, I see what you mean. Well, Class Ones are those who've rated just under the stability line on the yearly checks. They're perfectly decent, most of them." He looked at Kil half-challengingly. "Most of them lead perfectly regular lives, unless they get a bad stroke of luck, or something. The Class Two's are those who've shown bad Stab ratings and either a criminal record or criminal tendency. That'd be where their name Crim comes from, of course. Then the Threes, the Potes—" again Marsk made his jerky-eye reconnoiter of his office.

"What about them?"

"The Potes are potentials," said Marsk. When Kil still looked blank, the thin man made an angry gesture with one hand. "Potential dangers to the world peace! You know!"

"No," replied Kil, bluntly.

"They're the ones who could—who could build a CH bomb or find somebody else who could build one, or locate Files and wreck it . . ."

"What do you mean, locate Files?" interrupted Kil. "Files is right here at Police Headquarters."

"Is it? Oh, is it?" There was a momentary flash of weak anger from the thin man. "You Class A's are all the same. You're on top of the world, so you never wonder about it. Well, for your information, here at World Police Headquarters is one place Files isn't. It's been hunted for plenty of times, believe me, in the last hundred years. And it's not here. Nobody knows where it is, except maybe some of the top men in the Police."

Kil had the effective memory of the typical mnemonic engineer. He went back through it to his secondary school classes in Civics.

"Five square miles," he said, "of computer, power plant, record space, integrators and power lines. You don't hide that in your kilt pocket."

"Then you tell me where it is!" Marsk's eyes were bright. "Why if I could find that out, I could be rich tomorrow. I—" he checked himself. "You go see the Ace King, like I said."

"I still don't understand it," said Kil, stubbornly. "Why Ace King?"

"Because he's the top—the head man!" cried Marsk. "There's only one in each Slum. He runs everything."

"They have to move like everybody else, I suppose," said Kil. "What if another comes along while he's there?"

"Then one goes, or one gets closed up."

"Closed up?"

"That's what the Unstabs say," Marsk gave a little, twitching smile. "It means they kill him. Don't look so shocked. That's why they're Unstab. What do you suppose started that riot in the Tokyo Slum yesterday—or don't you listen to the news?"

Kil shook his head and returned grimly to the important point.

"Anyway, this man can help me?"

"If he wants to," said Marsk. "An Ace King can do anything—except locate Files." He looked earnestly at Kil. "I'll throw in some free advice. Keep your mouth shut as much as possible while you're down there. And hold onto your temper with both hands. The Police crack down on them if they hurt one of us, but you're Stab, and they hate Stabs, particularly Class A. Just don't give them an excuse to get rough, and you ought to do all right."

"Thanks," said Kil, getting up. "I'll remember."

"That's all right," Marsk rose with him. "I'm Stab, too. After all, they aren't our kind of people; though some of them aren't too bad. But we Stabs have to stick together, after all." He followed Kil to the door. "Just go into any bar or night club down there and ask the bartender for the Ace King. And then sit down someplace where you'll be sort of out of the way until he sends for you."

Kil nodded. And went out.

"Good luck!" said the voice of Marsk as the door closed between them.

It was not hard to get to the Unstab Area, the Slum, which was, in fact, nothing more than an unmarked and arbitrary number of blocks, south of the city terminal. Riding in on one of the roadways and shivering a little in the sudden chillness of the night breeze, Kil wondered why he had never been to one before. There had been no particular reason to go; but on the other hand, for a Stab, there was never any reason to go. Neither Unstab people, nor Unstab amusements would be liable to hold any particular attraction for a Class A. Still, there was nothing of the ghetto about the area. The Stabs and the Police had not gotten together to force the Unstabs into these small pockets within the community. It had been the Unstabs themselves who had chosen to huddle off away from the rest. The remainder of the world was just as open to them as it was to the Stabs; as their Slums were to the Stabs. Yet there was little straying from either section of the social group.

Of course, it was a known fact that the Unstabs resented Stabs.

There were no signs marking a boundary. But the minute Kil crossed into Unstab territory, he was made aware of the fact by a number of little things. For one, as he had noticed from his hotel window earlier, patches of dim light and even of actual shadow could suddenly be seen ahead on the heretofore brightly lit street, down which the moving roadway was carrying him. For another, the fixed sidewalks bordering the roadway and extending over to the front of the buildings along the street, began to be peopled by occasional lounging figures, not groups stopping and chatting as they might have elsewhere in the city, but solitary individuals leaning against store fronts and watching those who passed with an air of wariness or calculation. The shops themselves had a dingy air; as if, without being actually unclean, which was almost an impossibility in modern times, they had somehow managed to reflect the strange dustiness and disorder within the minds of those who occupied them. Few people seemed to be about; and yet the public buildings murmured with life behind dark or shielded fronts. Signs in muted colors identified the entertainment spots. And it was into one of these, a bar, that Kil left the safety of the moving roadway to enter.

To his surprise, and in contrast to the glowing sign out front, the door that opened to his Key revealed a place seemingly dead and all but deserted. As he stood just inside the entrance, blinking in the sudden and unaccustomed gloom, it became slowly apparent that this first impression was a mistake, fostered by darkness and silence. The place was thinly but evenly populated.

It was also larger than he had thought. To his left a short semi-circle of bar bellied out from the wall. To his right, a closely huddled pack of booths and tables faded off into the obscurity of a further wall that, for some reason, was broken up into little niches and crannies housing single booths in deep shadow. A scattering of dim forms sat here and there at the tables and there was a slim, irregular line of patrons around the bar.

With all this, it took only a short moment for Kil to understand what had caused him, instinctively, to check his entrance a few feet inside the front door. He had stepped not only into darkness, but also into that same silence, noted earlier, the

peculiar pregnancy of which is in itself a warning.
And now, in the whole place, there was not a
whisper, not a rustle, not a clink.

They sat or stood, he saw now with clearing
eyes, all staring at him. There was a tribal unanim-
ity in their motionlessness, an ancient tribal hos-
tility toward the stranger. They waited, it seemed,
for him to make the first move; and he, half-
hypnotized by the impact of their numerous eyes,
stood fixed and incapable.

Abruptly the silence was shattered by a wild,
drunken whoop. A tall, blond boy of less than
twenty, with a mop of unruly hair, staggered clear
of the bar and stood facing Kil, half the length of
the room between them.

"Well, big S!" he shouted. "Big S! B . . . ig,
dir . . .ty S!"

Kil did not move. The silence in the rest of the
bar continued unbroken. The boy stood weaving,
silent now, but not turning back to his drink.
Abruptly, the paralysis holding Kil snapped. He
turned himself slowly toward the other drinkers
watching him from the bar. He went down along it
to an open space opposite the bartender and
leaned across the bar to face him.

The bartender said nothing.

"I'd like," said Kil, "to talk to a man known as
the Ace King."

"A juby rig," said the man to Kil's right, suddenly. "I'll pipe."

The bartender looked at the man and then back
to Kil. His eyes were unfriendly.

"A stick," he said. His voice was harsh and
heavy, coming from a harsh and heavy face.

"If he is," said the man on Kil's right, "who do

you think you're coving with the gabby low?" He turned to Kil, a tall, cadaverous man with a dark Latin-looking face and something sardonic and distant in his eyes. "Who sent you, Chief?"

"Cole Marsk."

"Never heard of him."

"He's a private detective. I wanted him to do some work for me," said Kil. "He said he couldn't, but to see a man called the Ace King."

The tall man turned to the bartender.

"Spin the dosker, Joel," he said.

The bartender reached down below the bar and did something with his hands. He watched intently for a moment, then raised his head.

"Marsk's on," he said. "He's piped before."

"I'll pipe on then." The tall man turned once more to Kil. "Stay here until I come back for you. Sit at one of the tables there and keep your mouth shut."

He shoved his drink away and started toward the door.

"Hey, don't forget my per," yelled the bartender after him. "If it's a juby rig I want my five."

The tall man laughed derisively.

"You'll get five in a fist," he threw back over his shoulder without pausing. "Give him a drink and don't poison him. I'm piping this."

He went out the door. The bartender turned a bitter face back toward Kil.

"Well, what'll it be, *Chief*?" He spat the words out. Kil held on to his own temper with an effort.

"Nothing," he answered. He turned and strode across the room to a table in the shadows. He sat down. Away, at the far end of the bar, the mop-headed boy pivoted unsteadily to face him.

"Big, dirty, S!"

"Clab it!" shouted the bartender, turning on the youth. Muttering, the boy twisted back to his drink; and the rest of the customers, as if all actuated by a single circuit, turned likewise, ignoring Kil.

Kil sat and waited. Occasionally new people came in to the bar and others went out. The clientele changed faces without changing either numbers or types. Kil could have been invisible for all the attention paid him. He sat in stillness, feeling the waiting drain the tension from him, leaving him almost empty. For the moment, the hot coal of his purpose smothered and dimmed under the smoky pall of a dull and heavy apathy. He sat in a timeless vacuum, waiting for the tall man to return. Then, finally, after an interminable time, he came gradually back to conscious awareness, pricked by a faint whisper that was just reaching his ear.

"Chief . . . oh, Chief . . ."

Kil slowly raised his head and started to twist about to the table behind and to his left, which sat in one of the little wall niches in deepest shadow.

"No, Chief!" hissed the whisper, urgently. "Don't turn around. Keep looking the way you are. And don't move your lips when you answer."

Kil complied. He let his head droop as if tired; and with his face half-hidden, whispered back through still lips.

"Who're you?"

"Dekko, Chief."

"Dekko?"

"Dekko. I called you at the Stick gate yesterday. You remember. You were climbing into a cab and

I asked if you wanted a runny."

Slowly there swam back into focus in Kil's mind the picture of a narrow face, pointed-chinned and with straight black hair, which had grimaced at him through the window of the cab.

"You're that little man," said Kil. "Well? What do you want?"

"Work for you, Chief. You need a runny. I'm a good one."

Kil considered the answer for a second.

"What's a runny?" he whispered.

"A runner, Chief. I can run you anywhere. You got a problem. I can help. I got a talent; and I know all the wires."

"I don't," hissed Kil, exasperatedly, "understand half of what you're saying."

"That's it. You see, Chief?" The answering whisper was triumphant. "You don't know anything about anything. You're a lost juby in riggertown. If you hadn't been piped to Crown One, they'd be all over you in this place by now. How you going to get done what you got to get done without a runny to slip the wires for you? You'd get shook out every time you turned around until there wasn't nothing to shake out no more and then some Crim would come along and close you up."

"I don't think so," replied Kil. "I'm just down here to talk to this Ace King man. After that I'll be getting out."

"That's what you think, Chief. I watched you go into the Sticks and I read you coming out. You got a problem and it goes under the line where the wires are. I know. I tell you—"

The whisper stopped abruptly, as if the speaker

had choked it off in his throat.

"What do you know—" Kil was beginning, when out of the corner of his eye, he saw the tall, cadaverous man reentering the bar. He watched the other stride toward him until he stood over Kil at the table.

"All right, Chief," the tall man said. "Come on with me. Ace'll see you and I'm taking you to him."

Slowly, Kil rose to his feet. The tall man turned and led the way out of the bar. As he stepped away from the tables, Kil turned a little sideways and threw one quick glance back over his shoulder.

The table in the niche behind him was empty. Several tables down, a fat and drunken old man dozed above his half-finished drink. Otherwise the space surrounding where he had sat was deserted. There was no sign of the little man called Dekko anywhere in the place.

CHAPTER FOUR

THE tall man led Kil through several streets and finally down a dark alley to a building's side entrance. Within, there were several doors to be opened by the tall man's Key, and several short hallways to pass before they stepped at last into a long room stripped bare to the basic metal and plastic of its wall, ceiling and floors. The room was empty of furniture except for a desk at its far end, behind which a small man sat staring fixedly at them as they came in, and a chair before it. Behind the little man at the desk, another, younger man, in white tunic and kilt edged in gold, leaned against the opaqued window that filled that end of the room, looking pallid and almost macabre against its blackness.

"Here he is, Ace," said the tall man.

"Thank you, Birb. Ono, go stand by the door, will you?" As the man lounging against the window moved forward and around the desk, the man known as the Ace King kept his eyes fixed on

Kil. "So this is the man," he said, in a dry, hard voice that had a nearly feminine waspishness to it. "Well, come here and sit down, you."

Kil strode forward. The room was longer than it seemed. The bare walls and bright, unrelieved lighting gave it a hot, unnaturally clear and sharp appearance, like an hallucination seen in deep fever. As he reached the chair and sat down, Kil saw that the Ace was not sitting behind his desk, after all, but standing; and that he was much smaller than he had at first appeared. He was a square, dry-skinned man in his early fifties, swaddled almost, in long trousers of thick, purple cloth clipped into black boots and a black, turtle-necked long sleeved tunic. His lined face was leathery, his eyes small and hard.

"What's your name?" said the Ace.

Kil told him. The Ace stood looking at him.

"Well?" snapped the little man, at last, "Well? What did you want to see me about?"

Kil remembered Marsk's advice and took a firm grip on his temper with both hands.

"I want to find my wife," he answered. "She's disappeared. A private detective named Marsk said you might be able to help me."

"Oh, he did? Well, I've never even heard of him." The Ace frowned down at his desk and made a minute adjustment in the papers laid out in militarily precise order there. "However, since you're here, I might as well listen. What happened? I suppose you had some little lover's spat."

Kil felt himself go hot, and his eyes burned. With an effort, he held his voice down, though the words came out before he could stop them.

"Don't let the situation go to your head," he said. "I'll tell you what you're going to need to know."

There were a couple of audible breaths from the back of the room and Ace jerked his head up. The expression on his face as he stared at Kil did not change; but he went momentarily and horribly pale. After a short moment, his color came back.

"Go ahead," he said in a neutral voice.

Kil told him. In the retelling of it, he regained his calmness; and by the time he was finished he was once more in control of himself. As for Ace, he seemed almost friendly, as if the small passage-at-words had never been.

"Interesting," he said, when Kil had finished. "A strange story."

Kil looked sharply at him, to see if there was any further sarcasm in this, but the man's face was clear.

"Well?" demanded Kil.

"Well—what?"

"Can you find her?"

"Well, now," said the Ace. "That depends." He came around the desk and perched on a corner of it, looking down into Kil's face. "You come here to ask a service, you know," he said, softly. "You come here to see me because none of your Class A, or Class B, or Class C friends can help you."

"Friends?" echoed Kil. "I want to hire somebody. Can you do it? How much?"

The Ace stood up again and went back behind the desk. He sat down and it became immediately apparent that the chair to his desk had been abnormally cushioned, because he was nearly as tall seated as he had been standing.

"How much? Yes, how much?" he said. "That's right, you wouldn't want favors. But I feel generous, you know. There's actually several ways you could pay for my assistance."

"Check? Cash? It doesn't matter."

"No, no, you don't understand. Nothing like that. I said several ways, several different kinds of payments."

"Such as?" demanded Kil.

The Ace put his fingertips on the desk and leaned forward.

"Perhaps you know something that might be useful to me. It's an axiom of mine that valuable information is like diamonds, often stumbled upon unexpectedly. And since the price for what you want is high . . ." He let his voice trail off.

"How high?"

"Quite high. I might even say—by your standards—very high. There's people to be paid all over the world. You see, what we do is pass the word; and everybody in our areas the world over keeps his eyes open. So the price for the one who first discovers your wife has to be enough to make it worth the trouble of his looking. Then the local Ace in the area where she's discovered will want a slightly greater amount and naturally, you pay me the most of all."

"*How much?*" said Kil.

"But I'm just talking about money! Suppose you were able to pay some other way entirely, by providing me with information. Let's look on the optimistic side first." He held up two fingers of his right hand. "If you can help me with either one of two questions, we'll find your wife for nothing. *I'll* pay for it."

Kil stared at him for a long moment.

"All right," he said at last. "Ask ahead."

"That's nice," said the Ace, leaning back. "That's very agreeable. Now, for question number one. There is a man in whom we're all very interested. Is he a man? I think so. Yes, I think we can take that much for granted. Perhaps, talking to your letter-Class friends you've heard of him. Perhaps even met him. The Commissioner?"

The last words were said in almost an idle tone, so lightly and so casually that Kil staring at the short Unstab, had trouble for a moment believing that he had heard correctly.

"Who?" he asked.

"The Commissioner," repeated the Ace, blandly.

"I don't know anyone by that title."

"Now," said the Ace, "I can hardly believe that. He's one of your own people."

"What do you mean, one of my people?" snapped Kil.

"What people have you? The Class A's, of course."

"I don't know what you're talking about," said Kil.

"All right," the Ace sighed. "I'll be plain about it. You Class A's need the Police to stay where you are—on top of the world. You can't control the Police very well with a new head going in every six months, so you have a secret head man who goes by the title of Commissioner—an unofficial head. I want to know who he is."

"You're crazy!" said Kil, incredulously.

"You won't tell me?"

"I don't know; there is no such man."

"All right," the Ace's voice hardened. "It seems you don't want this wife of yours back as much as you say you do. But I'll give you another chance. What do you know about Sub-E?"

"Sub-E?"

The Ace sat and stared at him for a long, long moment without speaking.

"You know," he said at last. "You might just be telling the truth. You might just be the complete fool you seem to be, after all."

"Now, look!" Kil started up in his chair and felt hard hands slam him down again. He twisted his head to look behind him and saw the tall, cadaverous man, Birb, standing over him.

"You look," said the Ace, and Kil turned his eyes back to look at him. "You come in here and demand to see me, with your insufferable Class A nose in the air. You say you're going to tell me all I'll need to know—as if you were the one to be giving orders around here. As if I was dirt under your feet because you're Class A and I'm Class One. Never mind the fact that I've got more intelligence that you ever dreamed of having! Never mind that I could buy and sell you a thousand times over and never even notice the cost! Never mind—" The man's eyes were showing their whites all the way around the pupil and a little moisture flew from his working lips into Kil's face "—that I'm a busy man and your lousy little wife means nothing to me. You came in to see me. So let's talk business. Let's talk money, since you obviously haven't got anything else. How much will it cost to find your wife? How much will it cost in money? Two hundred thousand, that's what it'll cost!"

Kil blinked at the rigid little man, stunned.

"Two hundred thousand?" he managed, finally.

"Two hundred—*hundred* thousand! That's the price! That's the regular price! If you'd gone to any other Ace but me, they'd have asked you if you had that much money before they bothered to talk to you. But I wanted to be kind. I tried to be decent. I know mnemonic engineers aren't rich; and I tried to think of some way you could pay otherwise."

"Listen!" said Kil; but the words pouring from the Ace's mouth overwhelmed and flooded over his interruption.

"But no matter what I did, no matter what I tried, you continued to insult me, to try to take advantage of me! You planned this. You thought you could walk all over me because you're Class A and I'm Class One! You thought maybe you could bully me, scare me into working for you for nothing. Well, you've come to the wrong man for that! I've got position and authority. I've got power and I know it. If you'd been halfway decent I'd have found some way to help you. Two hundred thousand is twenty years' income to you, but it's nothing to me. I might even have paid part of it out of my own pocket just to be kind, to help you. But no matter how I tried, how I leaned over backwards to help you, you just trampled on me some more. Well, now you can go to hell! You can go to hell! You and your slut of a wife who's probably off with some other man right this very min—"

It was a wide desk, but Kil went over it in one jump. His hands closed around the soft, knitted fabric of the Ace's turtle-necked tunic, the desk chair flopped over backwards and they crashed to the floor together, the little man underneath, squalling like a cat. Through a dark blur of rage, Kil was conscious of blows landing on him from behind, of hard hands pulling him away from his enemy; but he held on grimly, until something broke in splintering pain against the back of his head and a black mist closed around him.

When it cleared a second later, there was water dripping from his face and he was being held upright between Birb and Ono. The Ace was facing him, his tunic torn and his face congested above it.

"Take him out," he said, breathing hard and speaking softly. "Take him out. Teach him to hit me!"

The two men dragged Kil away.

They went back out the route by which Kil had entered, and emerged into the alley. The sudden dimness, after the bright lights of the office and the corridors, was startling. At the far end of the alley the sunbeam-illuminated street was a distant rectangle of white light with black patches of shadow that were doorways pacing off the distance down the side of the building toward it.

"Hold him, Ono," said Birb.

There was a subtle shifting of hands and Kil found himself held in a full nelson by Ono, while the cadaverous man moved around to face him.

"All right, Stab," said Birb.

It was like the tail end of a bucking log in the rapids of a mountain stream catching him in the stomach. Kil doubled over, gasped for air and began to struggle. Other blows came swiftly and heavily. Body, head, neck, face, groin. There was a drumming in his ears and a haze of pain rose to blind him.

"Drop him." It was the voice of Birb again; and, although he had not been conscious of falling, Kil felt the hardness of the alley pavement rough against his cheek.

"Boots, Ono, and I'll—"

Suddenly, from nowhere, the universe rocked to a soundless flash of light and one of the two men above Kil screamed like a wounded horse. There was a scrambling sound in the alley and a series of long, hoarse gasps. Kil felt arms pulling him to his feet. Blindly he groped, his eyes still seared and sightless from the flash. Hands took his arm and pulled him, staggering, along.

"Can you run, Chief?" asked a voice. "Come on, hang onto me. We got to go fast."

It was the voice of Dekko.

CHAPTER FIVE

THE apartment was just like any apartment in the class of buildings which could be registered in with three weeks or more time to go on your Key; by which piece of evidence, coupled with the fact that by manners and language he was obviously Unstab, Kil came early to the conclusion that Dekko was Class One; by Files' rating, at least, the equal of the little man known as the Ace King. The apartment itself consisted of a sleeping room and lounge with lavatory off to one side and a small dining area, furnished with delivery slots, leading from the building's automatic kitchen. There was the usual furniture in the form of tables, beds, chairs, a vision box in each room and a large, wall-sized one-way window in the lounge. The first two days, when it was all Kil could do to drag his aching body on occasional trips between the bed and the lavatory, he had spent most of his waking hours lying on one of the beds and watching the bedroom screen. He occupied himself with news broadcasts, mainly, except for the occasions when the discomfort of his battered frame became too insistent a drag on his attention. Then he would switch over to one of the pain-relieving hypnotic patterns and give himself ten minutes of conditioning. The patterns were not too successful. He was a bad hypnotic subject and had known it since grade school. But at the same time he had a slight block against chemical palliatives, hating to surrender any level of his awareness to a drug; and he had turned down Dekko's offer of barbiturates.

The news broadcasts were the best distraction. He had never really listened to them before, and would not have listened to them now except that music or the regular light entertainment of the boxes left his mind too free to wander—and it wandered in only one direction. Ellen. Her going and her reasons for it had worn a deep, circular rut in his mind, around which he endlessly chased a question mark. The very instinct for self preservation steered him away from it now. And the news broadcasts helped. He was astonished, now that he listened, to discover that there was so much amiss in the world. While there were no big disasters—for which, of course, everyone could thank science—the number of small turbulences and revolts and accidents was so great that they were totalled up in kind and reported as statistics. There were statistics for everything. It seemed all you had to do was choose the appropriate percent of the population to which you belonged; and your individual group trouble was there waiting for you. The only exception seemed to be the Class

A's like himself. Not like himself, he corrected the thought in his head.

He wondered about Dekko, who was gone most of the time. The little man slipped in and out of the apartment like a sneak thief, making brief appearances to see that nothing was wanting for Kil, and immediately vanishing again. He either had someplace else to sleep, or slept nearly not at all.

The afternoon of the third day, however, Kil had dragged himself, grunting, from the bed to the lounge, and was sitting there, enjoying his first view of sky and city through the window, when the door to the apartment clicked open and Dekko's voice spoke cheerfully behind him.

"Hi, Chief. How's it mending?"

Kil turned his head and watched the small man approach.

"Better," he said.

Dekko closed the door behind him and came gliding across the carpet to drop in a chair opposite. He had a curious way of walking, almost on his toes, so that he moved with deceptive swiftness and a seemingly effortless stride. Seated, he was less imposing. His black hair was combed straight back above his abnormally wide forehead and sharp nose. The slight hump in his back thrust his shoulders and neck forward, so that his sharp chin seemed about to dig holes in the scarlet tunic covering his chest. His waist was small, but the forearms and calves that the tunic and kilt left uncovered were corded with surprising muscle.

He grinned at Kil.

"You stood up pretty well to being shook out," he said.

"Is that what you call it?" grunted Kil.

"Sometimes," said Dekko, his black eyes bright. "About time we talked things over, Chief."

Kil stirred restlessly, sending a twinge through his still-stiff middle.

"Look," he said. "Can we do without the Chief? It makes me feel like something dug up out of a museum. The name's Bruner, or Kil if you like that better."

"Do me!" said Dekko. His eyes were black, bright, humorous points in his face. "Kil, then; though it's not usual for a runny."

Kil examined him.

"Tell me something," he said, "What is usual for a runny? Does a runny usually do the sort of thing you've had to do for me?"

Dekko went off into a perfectly silent fit of laughter. He sat in the chair with his thin shoulders shaking.

"Do me, no!" he said. "I'm a free-lance."

"I don't get it."

"Ordinary runnies," explained Dekko, "got to check out with their Ace, wherever they are. A free-lance like me doesn't give a damn for Ace or anybody. That's the difference."

Kil bent a little toward him in curiosity.

"How do you get to be a free-lance?"

Dekko flashed a mouthful of perfectly even teeth.

"You need something special." He smiled at Kil. "And don't ask me what I got. That's a trade secret. All you need to know is that I can deliver where maybe an ordinary runny can't."

Kil shook his head and leaned back.

"I don't think you can, in my case," he said.

"You don't know what I'm up against."

"Sure. Wife's gone," said Dekko.

Kil jerked upright again in surprise.

"How did you know?"

Dekko held up three fingers.

"Three people you told your yarn to. I saw you go into the Sticks and I read you for a problem. I saw you come out the Stick gate and you still had the problem, so you told the Sticks and they didn't help. I checked you across the city and into a hotel; I checked you out of the hotel to see a two-bit named Marsk. I checked you into the area to see Ace. That's three. Some Stick, Marsk, and Ace. Now you tell me who told me."

"Marsk," said Kil, without hesitation. "But what's a Stick?"

"A Nightstick—a World Cop."

"What's a Nightstick?"

Dekko laughed again.

"The way I heard it," he said. "Once there was cops that carried clubs called nightsticks. Nobody was supposed to stand still on the streets in those days. If you did, some cop with a nightstick'd come up and tell you to move on. Get it now?" He peered at Kil.

"Oh." said Kil. "You mean this business of the World Police making sure everybody moves on from the area he's in, when his permitted time is up?"

"That's it: Sticks."

Kil nodded and went back to his own problem. "What makes you think you can do something for me when nobody else can? And what's your price, anyway? I can't pay two hundred thousand dollars."

"Who asked it? That's Ace price," said Dekko. "With me you don't pay a price because you're not buying, you're hiring. I cost a thousand a month; and I'm worth it. To answer that first question, though, I don't know whether I can get your wife back or not. But I know stuff nobody else does; and I've got a wire."

Kil shook his head bewilderedly.

"I don't understand half what you're saying. What's this wire business?"

"The Societies. I'm Thieves Guild and a couple of other things. We can try running a wire to the O.T.L. and check through them."

"What's—" said Kil and stopped. "I'm sorry to keep asking what things are, but this is all Greek to me."

"Sure," answered Dekko. "You're an A. Stab. And A. Stabs don't know anything, in spite of what most of the riggers think. Just sit back and listen and I'll explain it."

Kil nodded.

"Forget Ace—any Ace," said Dekko. "Aces are all little frogs in little puddles. There's only two big outfits in the world today. One's the Sticks. The other's made up out of the Societies."

"Societies—" frowned Kil. "Now, it seems to me I heard something about a Society once."

"There's thousands of them," said Dekko. "They're secret, most of them. Most harmless, but some aren't. People, you see, need something, with Files making them shift every few weeks or months. Files has set things up this last hundred years so no groups can get together and want to fight other groups. That's fine to keep the peace, but its lonely for the single ones. You never know anybody for long. Wife, maybe, and kids while they're growing up and living with you; but when you got to keep moving, you fall apart easy. You can't even get to liking the place you live, or your job, because in just a little while you're going to trade it all for a place and a job just like it—but different—maybe halfway around the world."

"But look here—" began Kil.

"Let me finish. So along comes a Society, any old Society, and you join up. You get accepted, you wear something that shows you're accepted, and you know what to look for on somebody else. You hit a new place and start looking around. You see somebody wearing the same gimmick you've got; you go up to him and you're in. You got a friend, maybe not a real close friend, but it's not like being a stranger all the time, so much."

"But why secret?" asked Kil, when Dekko stopped.

"Makes it stronger. Usually you pledge yourself to all sorts of things: treat anyone else in the Society like a brother, whether you know him or not. Some go further. In some Societies, if a fellow member asks for anything you got, you got to give it to him, no questions asked."

Kil shook his head.

"I can't understand why I never heard of all this before," he said.

"You're A. Stab.," repeated Dekko. "A. Stabs. are the only ones that don't need all this stuff because they're the only ones that're adjusted. They fit this crazy world of Files."

"Sometimes," said Kil, thinking of Ellen.

"Yeah, sometimes," agreed Dekko. "Now listen, there's more to it than that. There's all kinds of different Societies, but there's only one O.T.L. Now don't ask me what the letters stand for, because I don't know. Maybe even the O.T.L.'s themselves don't know. But O. T. L.'s about forty years old and it sits right at the head of all the other Societies. All the important ones got members who're members of O.T.L. O.T.L. can do anything, except find Files. They can probably find your wife." He paused, a little significantly. "Ever think she might be a member of something herself?"

"A member?"

"Of some Society."

"No, of course—I don't think—" Kil dwindled off on a doubtful note.

"It sounds like it. That old man coming up—"

"Wait!" cried Kil. "I think I've got something. I mentioned it to that man McElroy at the Police Headquarters, but he didn't believe me. Is there any Society that doesn't wear Keys?" He stopped before something strange and brilliant and unfathomable in Dekko's eyes.

"Society without Keys?" said Dekko. "Are you psycho, Kil? How could anyone live, Society or no Society, without a Key, even if the Police'd let them? You were—what makes you think there's something like that?"

"The old man who took Ellen away hadn't any Key on his wrist."

"You were looking at the wrong arm."

"No," said Kil stubbornly. "No, I wasn't."

"Then you hit a blind spot. Listen," Dekko leaned forward earnestly. "Everything in this world's got a door, right?"

"Yes," admitted Kil, grudgingly.

"And every door's got a cup? And you can't open that door without a Key to put in that cup. If you didn't have a Key, it'd be like being in a city when your time was up. You couldn't open anything. You couldn't get in to eat, or sleep, to get clothes, or draw money or anything. That's why Files was set up the way it was. Anyone who overstays their time in any one spot got to move or die. If there was any way around it, there wouldn't be any point to Files."

"The transportation system's open. You don't need a Key to take a rocket, or a mag ship," said Kil.

"What good's that to you? So you can go to another city. But that city's closed, too. Listen to me, Kil, if you don't have a Key, there's a billion doors closed against you. You're locked out; locked out of all the world!"

Kil shook his head stubbornly.

"I saw it," he said.

"Sure, think that if you want," Dekko straightened up. "How about it? You want to try stringing a wire to the O.T.L.? Do you want to hire me?"

Kil nodded.

"You're hired," he said. "How do we start?"

"Pasadena, California; then the Thieves Guild, first," said Dekko. "You got to join, you know. Then some other Society, one of the big ones. Then, if we can do it, the O.T.L."

Kil got stiffly to his feet.

"All right," he said. "I guess I'm good enough to travel." Dekko went off into another of his silent fits of laughter.

"Why, Kil," he said, when he had sobered again, "you don't just walk out the door and out of riggertown like that. Don't you remember? Ace was having you shook out when I came along and shorted out a pocket sunbeam in the eyes of those two crims of his. The word's still out for you. We're going to have to change the way you look and a lot more about you if we want to make it to the Terminal without trouble."

"We do?" said Kil. "Well, let's get busy at it, then."

"Do me!" Dekko grinned at him. "You got a lot to learn."

During the next three days Kil came around to admitting this himself. But first came the matter of changing his appearance. The primary change Dekko insisted upon was bleaching Kil's hair to a silvery white.

"But you'll just make me that much more conspicuous," Kil protested.

"You've got the wrong idea," Dekko explained, patiently. "You want to look just like everyone else? You want to fade into the background? Sure, that's fine for people who aren't being looked for specially. But when you got someone who knows what you looked like to start off with, you want them to look at you now and then say, no, that couldn't possibly be the juby we're after."

"I still think—"

"No. Now listen. I got a hump on my back. One guess how people remember me? If I could get rid of that hump I could walk up to most of them tomorrow and they'd scratch their heads trying to remember what I remind them of. Now, you—you

change your hair to white. You stand out in a
crowd like a streetside sunbeam. But they take
one look at you and that's all they see—they see a
freak with white hair and a young face. The fact
your face is like what they're looking for makes
them all the more positive it's not you. Their mind
works backward. It starts making excuses for the
fact that you look like you. Ends up they're ready
to swear you don't look like what you actually
look like at all. It's like hiding something in plain
sight. They say, that can't be it. It's not hidden."

Kil gave in, with misgivings.

The next part was more complicated, Dekko
insisted on teaching him how to walk, talk and act
like an Unstab.

"Now, there's got to be something inside you,"
he instructed. "That part of it you should be able
to do all right because you got something inside
you; this business of your wife. But remember
that—that's the difference between Unstab and
Stab. An Unstab's got something inside him,
chewing on him all the time. So just start thinking
of your wife from the minute we step out the door
and keep it up."

Kil nodded.

"That won't be hard," he said.

"Now, about the way you act. Unstabs don't just
wander through the area not looking at anything.
They're out to make something, or keep what they
already made. They watch all the time, everything. Keep your eyes going and act suspicious of
anybody."

"Right," said Kil.

"You got one point in your favor. You can look

at someone as if you want to cut their guts out. Now, that's good for the average rigger you'll bump into because it fits down here. But if you run across anyone who saw you before you saw Ace, watch your face, because they'll remember that expression as something special to you."

Kil sighed.

"I've been trying to control that all my life," he said.

"Well, now it's important Now, about the talk—the gabby low. This area here is riggertown; and everybody in it's a rigger—or thinks he is. When one rigger takes another for something, that makes the second rigger a juby. Anybody who doesn't know riggertown or gets rigged is a juby. Anybody who's Stab. is Big S. . . ."

"I'll never learn all that," said Kil. "It's like another language."

"You will," said Dekko, "if you want your wife back."

Finally, the fifth day after Dekko had brought him back to the apartment, they were ready.

"You go first," Dekko told him. "Now, you know the route to the Terminal. It's eight to one no one'll even look twice at you. But if there's trouble, just stall. I'll be about forty yards behind you and I'll come up and take care of it. I'll say that again. Wait for me. Clear?"

"What about you?" asked Kil. "What if someone recognizes you?"

Dekko laughed noiselessly.

"Nobody's seen me. Those two Crims of Ace's were blind before they knew what hit them. Let's roll it."

"They went out. After all this, the trip to the
Terminal was anti-climactic. No one so much as
looked at Kil.

CHAPTER SIX

It was different travelling, Kil found, after his recent experience with the Unstabs. That and the training session Dekko had put him through had had the effect of rendering him suddenly and almost painfully aware of the Unstab point of view. For the first time he knew what it felt like to be conscious of accepted society as something apart from himself. He felt it and something deep and rebellious within him resented it. He looked around at his fellow passengers, once the rocket had reached peak altitude and started its long glide toward the west coat, with naked eyes. Each individual struck him, for the first time, as a living enigma, a walking puzzle box of thought and flesh. What would this man do, or that woman, if Kil were to walk up to them this minute and tell them what had happened to him? Which ones were Unstab? Which ones were members of some Society or other? Which ones were, perhaps,

World Police out of uniform or on some secret duty? The normally homogeneous structure of society seemed to Kil suddenly broken, shattered into a million fragments—into four billion odd fragments—each one, one of the world's four billion odd population. And Ellen lost among them. Lost . . . lost . . . lost. . . .

They came down at the foot of the mountains in Pasadena, in the Arroyo Seco, where there had once been a famous stadium. And he and Dekko took a cab to the headquarters of the Thieves Guild, a large, rambling, temporary structure made of twenty-year plastic, high up on the side of the mountains. Inside the front door was an anteroom and a surprisingly beautiful blonde woman in early middle age. She and Dekko spoke together for a moment in low tones beyond Kil's hearing. Then she rose from the desk where she had been sitting and walked across the room to a door which she opened with her own Key.

"Go ahead," she said. "He's in." And she stood aside to let them pass. Following Dekko through the door, Kil caught his breath and stopped dead with an exclamation.

Sitting facing them in an oversized chair was a huge man with a completely bald head above a sad oriental face. He sat as if weary with the weight of his great body; and all the furniture of the room about him, like the chair he sat on, was built oversize, outsize, larger than human. The effect was not so much to strike the stranger with surprise at something so bizarre and unusual, as to make him feel that these overlarge proportions were in fact the true ones, and that it was he who was diminished, reduced, brought down to childhood's size again. Like children, Kil and Dekko approached the giant; but if this was not without its profound effect on Kil, it appeared to affect Dekko not at all.

"Kil," said Dekko, stopping before the chair. "This is Toy."

The obsidian eyes in the wide yellow face turned to focus on Kil.

"Yes, she's my wife," said Toy, without preamble, in a bass as heavy as himself. "I'll tell you that to satisfy your curiosity right from the start. She's my wife and she loves me. I don't know why. Any normal woman would have left me long ago."

Kil, startled and embarrassed by this unexpected attack, found himself suddenly wordless. He stared at the giant, caught too suddenly and unpreparedly to be angry. Dekko smiled.

"Fishing, Toy?" he asked.

"Only observing," replied Toy. "How many people do you think have come through that door or some similar door, and seen me and not wondered about her?" His eyes went back to Kil. "Excuse me. It's my one bitterness. Like King Midas who turned everything he touched to gold. Everything I touch," his huge right hand curled around the end of his chairarm and the tough plastic bent like cardboard, "turns to fragments."

He let go of the chair arm.

"Excuse me again," he said. "You've come at a bad time. I've been pitying myself. What can I do for you?"

Dekko nodded at Kil.

"Him," he said, succinctly.

"Him?" echoed Toy. The black eyes took in Kil for a long moment. "You look as if you had a problem, young man. How do you like it—this world, this ant-swarm, this mechanized midden heap, this modern age of ours? Does it suit you? Can you find accomplishment in our better mousetraps, art in our improved plumbing, glory in our conquest of bloodless mathematics, and adventure in our antiseptic, well-lighted and air-conditioned vice dens? What purposeful lives we lead in our inoculated trottings to and fro about the world. Don't you agree?"

"It looks like you don't," said Kil.

"Me?" said the giant. "I'm an anachronism. No, by God, I flatter myself. I'm a living fossil, a most excellent specimen of Tyrannosaurus Rex, claws clipped, teeth capped, and set to holding hanks of yarn for old ladies with knitting on their mind. I'm a superb body in an age when bodies have gone out of style. What a successful chieftain, what an outstanding hero I would have made at any time up to the last few hundred years, before the world became so cluttered up. What a Khan, what a Varanger, what a Viking I would have been. Just think, I could have been a Greek legend, like Hercules, or a Roman Emperor of the Legions like Magnus Maximus. No, forget fame. Think just what a happy cave man I would have made. I can break the neck of a bull with one twist of my arms; what an excellent provider of meat for my tribe. I can handle a bow with a three hundred and fifty pound pull and send an arrow more than a mile. What a pillar of strength in time of trouble. And modesty forbids that I tell you about my capabilities with a stone axe. You may possibly find me a trifle bitter; and you're correct. In a world of future-happy people, my future is all in the past."

Dekko shifted restlessly.

"How about it?" he said.

"Nothing. If she passed you, it's all right. What's your name, young man?"

"Kil Bruner," said Kil.

"Kil, there's only one requirement for entrance into the Guild. Once you're in, the Guild protects you and you're expected to help anyone in the Guild. None of this nonsense about what's mine is yours; and all you have is mine. But there's one condition. And that is, you have to think over the reasons for your entering for fifteen minutes, without speaking and without moving, while I watch you. If you still want to enter at the end of that time, you're in."

"That's all right," said Kil.

"Good. Come on, then." With astounding lightness, Toy rose to his feet; and now, standing, his great size was all the more apparent; for he was built thick and broad, with squat body and relatively short bow legs but standing his head towered more than a foot above Kil's. Kil looked at Dekko; Dekko did not move, except to gesture in Toy's direction. Kil turned and followed the giant.

Toy faced his Key into the cup of a further door that let them into a smaller room. It was not small as rooms go, but Toy filled it. It was bare of furnishings except for two chairs, one built to Toy's outsize dimensions, another of normal proportions. The large chair sat off to one side; and the smaller faced a far wall on which was a large clock whose second hand crept slowly around the face.

"Sit down," said Toy, taking the large chair.
"And think."

Kil settled himself. He was aware of the giant
lolling back and regarding him, but Toy was not
directly in his line of vision and Kil made no
attempt to look at him. Instead, he sat back and
looked at the clock.

The second hand was moving around the dial,
with the inexorable slowness of all second hands.
It made no sound, and there was no sound
elsewhere in the room. Toy moved not at all, and
even the sound of his breathing was inaudible to
Kil's ears. Kil watched the clock.

He had not really intended to think. He had
accepted and dismissed this minor ordeal in the
same moment. It was merely, he thought, a matter
of sitting still for fifteen minutes, and that would
be all. He found it was not that simple.

Slowly, the seconds began to stretch out.
Though he knew that in fact no such thing was
happening, it seemed that the second hand was
beginning to slow its crawl. His body, at first
comfortable, began to protest against its forced
inactivity. The sound of his own breathing, the
sound of his heart beating, grew larger in the
stillness until they seemed to thunder in his ears.
Little itches and cramps came and went and mul-
tiplied in mounting protest until they threatened
to force him to move in spite of all his will.

He saw the danger now. Grimly, he set himself
to combat it, and the clamoring hordes of the
body, defeated, drew back and relapsed into silence. Before his fixed eyes, the hands of the clock

had marked off only a little more than four minutes.

And now, with the body out of the way, came a new assault upon his self-control. The mind, which had been lying quietly inactive during these first few minutes, now began to stir itself with little fears and doubts.

Why was this test? What was he doing here? Was he actually taking the right way to solve his problem? The rising tide of his thoughts swept him inexorably to the heart of his troubles. He had not intended to think about it, but now his mind ran free like an unleashed hound; and he realized suddenly that this was the true test, that the will power that had gained him his victory over a rebel body could be no help with this. The doubts and fears came thick and fast. His vision seemed strangely blurred as if he were on the verge of passing into unconsciousness; and through it he could see, in contrast to his racing thoughts, a second hand on the wall clock that seemed almost to have stopped.

Now, to add to this, he became suddenly and painfully conscious of the eyes of Toy upon him. He could not turn his head and see those eyes; but he felt them boring like twin scalpels probing the buzzing wasp's nest of his brain. The pressure rose intolerably within him and he knew, suddenly, that unless he found some avenue of escape for it, soon, the tension would become too much for him and he would speak or move, would jump to his feet and run from the room.

Desperately, he searched within himself for some final source of strength. *For Ellen,* he thought, *Ellen.* And then he found, in the thought of Ellen herself, what he was looking for. It rose up before him like a vision of cool water and he sank down into it, gratefully.

Because it was for Ellen, of course. Out of the harsh and senseless tangle of a paradoxical world with its Unstabs, its Police, its Societies, its problems large and small, the fact of his love and his longing for his wife rose as one clear and simple truth. Whatever else might be right or wrong, this was right. It was right that he should want her. It was wrong that she should have been taken away from him. And it was right that he go after her, by any means, by all means, until he found her. Whatever else he might do that was wrong, this that he did, was right. Ellen . . . Ellen . . . and the little, bittersweet memories of her came back, a touch in the darkness, beside him in the night time, a distant, half-heard bustle of movement elsewhere in their apartment as he worked, and drew him into them, away from the room and Toy and the clock and everything. . . .

"Kil."

Kil came back with a start and sat up.

"What—" he said. "The fifteen minutes up?"

"Forty minutes are up," answered Toy. There was a curious look on his face, a strange look of mixed sympathy and interest. "I'd have liked to wait longer; but we've got Dekko to consider. Before we go back, though, is there anything you might like to tell me?"

"No," said Kil, slowly. "No, I don't think so."

"Maybe I'm wrong," said Toy, "but I get the impression that you may be one of those few lucky people who've found something worth fighting for. It's what I've looked for all my life and never found." His voice had gone bitter again. "It's impossible to cut yourself on the tinfoil edge of existence nowadays. If I could just find something of the sort you've—well, never mind. But if you ever need help that I could give, you might ask me for it, if you feel like it. And I might even give it."

"Thanks," Kil looked at him. For a short moment they looked at each other, unsmiling.

Toy grunted, and got up, and led the way back to the other room. Dekko was waiting there for them; and he looked at Kil curiously as they appeared. Toy went across to a cabinet in the wall and took from it a wrist band.

"Let's see your Key," he said. Kil gave it to him; and the yellow faced man's large fingers deftly detached it from its old wrist band and pinched it into the new one he had taken from the cabinet. He held it close to the Key on his own wrist and lifted both to Kil's ear together. A tiny, high-pitched hum could be heard coming from both instruments.

"That's it," he gave the Key back to Kil, who slipped it back on his wrist. "That's our identification. Any two Keys of Guild members brought together will hum like that. Also, before they hum, there's a vibration you'll feel in the skin of your wrist, so that you can make identification without attracting undue attention, if you want."

"I'm a member now?" asked Kil.

"You're a member," said Toy. "Anything else?"

"Yes," spoke up Dekko. "We want an in to one of the big Societies. Which ones are meeting soon?"

Toy sighed.

"So that's why you've come to me." He nodded, almost as if to himself. "There's a branch of the Panther meeting tonight.

Kil looked at him curiously.

"Do you belong?" he asked.

"No, but my wife does. She's a very useful woman." There was a hint of something like sadness in the giant's voice. "You'll have to wait until dark. Then she'll take you." He looked at Dekko oddly. "Sometimes I wonder about you," he said.

"Every man to his own trade, Chief," said Dekko, unperturbed.

"Yes—" Toy nodded. "Go out the way you came in. She'll take care of you."

And so they left him.

Toy's wife found them a room in the building and suggested that they rest until evening. Shortly after nightfall, she came for them and led them out to a garage. The cool coastal air blew about them as they got into a small personal flyer and the roof above them rumbled back to reveal the stars. As soon as they were in, Toy's wife closed the transparent canopy of the flyer, and opaqued it, taking a pair of depolarizing glasses from the flyer's glove compartment to insure her own vision, and putting them on.

"Sorry about this," she smiled at Kil below the twin darkness of the lenses. "Until you're accepted, the route to the meeting place has to be secret. We'll be there in about fifteen minutes."

They took off; and a quarter of an hour later the flyer came down with a soft thump, to roll for some little distance along a smooth surface. Then the woman stopped it and opened the canopy.

"Here we are, all out," she said.

She took his hand to lead him, and Kil felt a tingle travel through his spine. From that moment on, he later remembered nothing of his initiation into the Panthers, except for the vague feeling of having been wandering through a jungle. . . . Slowly the jungle faded about him. He came back to himself, standing in the draped and shadowy corner of a large room where people moved languidly about. Some sort of cocktail party seemed to be in progress. He crossed the room and got a drink, which he took thirstily. Then he went in search of Dekko, or Toy's wife.

Toy's wife was nowhere to be found, but he discovered Dekko in conversation with a thickset, gray-haired man in black tunic and kilt.

"I don't know," the gray-haired man was saying. "Nobody in the Duluth area at the moment that I know personally. It doesn't matter, I can give you two a visa, so they know you've been checked here recently, sir." He broke off, turning to Kil, as Kil came up.

"That's him," said Dekko.

"Oh yes; I'm Jacques Shriner, Mr. Bruner." The gray-haired man offered his hand, beaming out of a plump and ruddy face. "If you two'll come back to the office, I'll make out the visas."

He turned and led the way across the room to a small door. Facing his Key into the cup, he let them in and carefully closed the door behind them. They found themselves in a small business room furnished with a desk and microfile cabinet. Shriner went across to the desk and produced a couple of small, plastic disks, which he made out with their names and the date, signing each with his own name and thumbprint.

"Not that you need these—your arm marks are sufficient," he said, lifting his own arm, and Kil saw on it scratches like those a large cat might have made, and suddenly felt the sting of scratches on his own arm. "But just in case—"

"Thanks," said Dekko.

"Not at all," replied Shriner. "Enjoy yourselves in Duluth."

He beamed them out of his office and back to the party.

They crossed the room again to a further door that Dekko appeared to know about. It let them into a small, circular hallway where a bored-looking attendant stood. From this hallway, several exits led in different directions.

"Which one, Chief?" asked Dekko.

"Any one," replied the attendant. He was dressed in conventional dark slacks and a dramatically slashed tunic with a hoop collar, but there was an unusual glassiness about his appearance that drew Kil's attention. It was something just on the edge of visibility, like an almost perfectly transparent soap-bubble sort of film, just above the surface of his limbs and body. Then he turned so that Kil saw a heavy gasgun hanging at his side; and suddenly Kil recognized the glassiness as body armor of the phase shield type. He was confirmed in this recognition as the attendant waddled a few steps forward. The metal mesh supporting the shield under his clothing must be cruelly heavy.

Dekko, however, appeared to pay no attention

to the attendant and his illegal equipment; but
turned and vanished down the nearest tunnel entrance. Kil followed. A short distance on they
passed through a door and into a sort of cave that
ascended steeply.

"What's all this about Duluth?" asked Kil,
when they had gone some ways up the cave.

"Close to the top," answered Dekko. "Like any
business, you got to know what the competition's
doing. It's Stick headquarters, so headquarters of
everything else isn't far off. For us, that means the
O.T.L."

The cave had leveled off now. They went on a
short distance, opened a final door and stepped
out on a strip of shelving pebbly beach. Overhead,
gulls swooped, crying; the early morning sun
washed the ocean shore in white light. For a minute Kil felt shock to discover that his period of
hypnosis had lasted so long. Then this feeling was
lost forever in something greater that crept over
and buried it like an avalanche on some solitary
mountain climber—for he saw the sea.

Water—water. Water and Ellen—Ellen as she
had been the night she had gone away; and the
ocean then stretching wide and silver-dark to the
horizon. Like a man in a dream, Kil turned and
took one step toward the curling waves.

"Kil! *Kil!*" And then Dekko had him by the
arm, holding him back. For a moment he began a
half-convulsive struggle to free himself. Then the
spell snapped and he turned his back on the wide
sea.

And Dekko drew him away.

CHAPTER SEVEN

THEY took the noon rocket back to Duluth and found themselves a set of rooms in an unclassified hotel outside the Slums. That night they went to the Aurora, Duluth's largest entertainment center. Kil had already gone out during the afternoon to draw from his account and replenish his dwindling cash reserves. He drew three thousand for himself and an additional thousand for Dekko. It had occurred to him that the little humpback was still unpaid; and probably, therefore, in need of cash himself.

This could hardly have been the case. When he got back to the hotel, he found that Dekko had spent what could only have been a sizable amount on some evening clothes. These were not throwaways of plastic like their ordinary, daily dress, but trousers, tunic and short jacket of pressed silk. Their color was a heavy yellow, shot with black; a startling combination. And not only that, but the jacket was squared and stiffened with a high, hooped collar and boxed shoulders that all but disguised the fact of his hump.

Kil stared.

Dekko smiled. It was a different expression from his former grin, tight-lipped and a little sardonic.

"We're working a different territory from here on," he said. "I got you an outfit, too."

Kil followed his pointing finger and went to a closet recess. On the wire, he saw a kilt and tunic also of silk, scarlet tunic and scarlet and black checkerboard design, pleated kilt. A silver weapon belt holding a little dress gun and a silver-handle poniard went with it. A fourragère looped from one shoulder of the tunic, and a heavy ring, with a square-cut emerald hung by a thread from the wire.

Kil scowled blackly.

"You expect me to wear this?" he demanded. "I'll look like a damned pruce."

Dekko shook with silent laughter.

"Put it on," he said. "And get the dye out of your hair."

Growling, Kil got into the rig. When it was on, complete to the emerald ring on the index finger of his left hand, he examined himself in the mirror. The effect was not as bad as he had expected. He was undeniably overdressed, but a certain sort of genius seemed to have guided Dekko in his selections. Kil looked not so much affected as dissipated, in a dark and reckless way. His own harsh features took the curse off the prettiness of the costume.

"I still don't see why this—how much did it all cost?" he asked.

"Seven hundred and eighty for both," replied Dekko. "You can pay me." He looked at Kil. "Know anything about using a gun or a knife?"

"No."

"Good. Then you won't be tempted." Dekko accepted the money for the clothes and his own month's stipend. "Keep it on you now that you've got it on. I want you to get used to it."

They wore their new clothes down to dinner. It was not as bad as Kil had expected. People stared at him, but not with the accompanying snickers he had expected. By eleven that night, when they got to the Aurora, four hours wear and as many drinks had him all but reconciled to the figure he cut. He and Dekko paused at the edge of a crowded dance floor and Dekko consulted a waiter.

"All right, we got a table," he said, turning back to Kil.

Kil allowed himself to be drawn over to a table on the far edge of the dance floor. They sat down.

"Now what?" he looked at Dekko.

"We wait. Put your arm on the table, out in sight."

He had already done so himself. The white lines of his own scars were almost invisible in the shifting lights of the dance floor. Kil sighed and followed suit. His scratches, now scabbed over, stood out blackly against the tan skin. Dekko ordered drinks and they sat, sipping.

Before them the crowd swirled as dancing couples went by. Kil sat stiffly, expecting momentarily that some one of the spinning, weaving swarm before him would stop and speak. But it was not from the dance floor before them that recognition finally came, but from behind them. Abruptly, Kil felt a soft, warm breath on his cheek and slim fingertips reached around his shoulder to stroke gently the scratches.

"Oooh," sighed a soft voice. "Panther."

Kil turned to look up into the flushed, pretty face of a dark-haired girl in a brief green gown. Her shadowed eyes glistened with a strange excitement and the scent of perfumed wine was on her breath. Slowly, she lifted her arm, sliding it around his chest until he, looking down, saw the faint white scars of healed scratches also on her skin.

"Will you be there tonight?" she asked, softly.

Dekko said nothing; and after a second Kil realized it was up to him to ask.

"Where?"

"The Hill—at one this morning. Come to the cave beyond the pool in the jungle."

"The cave—"

"I'll wait for you—at the cave—panther—" Her hand slid back and away, across his chest. She slipped out of sight and into the crowd.

Kil, looking over across the table at Dekko, caught the little man's smile.

"All right," Kil said, harshly. "She said the Hill. How do we find out where that is?"

"I know," said Dekko.

Dekko did know. A little over an hour later they caught an aircab to the older area of the city, up on the hillside above Duluth. The cab set them down in front of an ancient building, sealed up and with the appearance of having been shut for some time.

"How do we get in?" Kil wanted to know.

Dekko did not answer. He was prowling along the side of the building. After a momentary hesitation, Kil followed him. The small man was testing the plastic seals of the ground floor windows as he went—apparently without success. But as Kil passed a window Dekko had already tested, the faintest of whispers came to his ears.

"*What is real?*"

Kil stopped.

"*Only,*" he said, the words coming from some dim memory, "*the jungle is real.*"

"*Brother, come in.*"

"Dekko!" called Kil, softly.

Dekko turned and came back. The plastic seal was already swinging inward, and they stepped through the opening into darkness.

"*Arms,*" said the voice.

A single shaft of white light stabbed down out of nowhere. There was no perceptible diffusion; merely one small area of brilliance, and all the rest in darkness. They extended their arms into the light and revealed their scars. The light winked out.

"*Enter into the jungle.*"

It was the same illusion over again, and this time Kil thought he probably could have thrown off the suggestion, but instead he allowed himself to slip part way under. For a while he roamed the jungle. . . . When a certain time had gone by, he pulled himself back to reality.

Again, as he came out of it, Kil found himself in the atmosphere of something like a polite cocktail party. The only differences from last time were that the place was larger and the guests more numerous. He threaded his way among them, indifferent except for one moment when, passing a curtained alcove, he caught sight of the dark haired girl who had spoken to him at the Aurora. She sat on a divan, leaning back with her eyes closed, obviously still under the hypnosis; and there was a look of loneliness and waiting on her face. A feeling of guilt and shame touched Kil; he turned quickly away.

Finally, he found Dekko. The little man was seated all by himself in a corner, holding a drink. His eyes flickered with shrewd alertness as Kil came up.

"Got it!" he said, as Kil sat down beside him.

"Got what?"

For answer, Dekko pointed through the shifting crowd to a tall, tanned, teen-aged-seeming girl with auburn hair.

"O.T.L.," he said briefly.

Kil stared in surprise. Of all things, he had not expected a girl. And she was beautiful. Just how beautiful became apparent in a moment when, swinging around to talk to someone else, her full face came into their line of vision. It was a face as flawless as the body to which it belonged, slim-featured and serene.

"Her name's Melee Alain," Dekko spoke softly in Kil's ear. "She's the one I dressed you up for."

"Dressed me—"

"Sure. What kind of bait do you think I'd make?" and Dekko rocked for a second with his silent laughter. "She's our wire to the O.T.L. She knows where they meet and she can invite us to wherever it is. That's what you've got to get her to do."

"I do?" said Kil. "I'm no good at that sort of thing."

"You've got to be. It won't be as hard as you think. Listen, she's a Class Two."

"Class Two?" Kil stared. "That girl? Criminally Unstab?"

"That's right. She's as much a Crim as those two of Ace's. She's got tangled circuits up top. That'll help us."

"How can anything like that help?" Kil was staring at the beautiful face in horror and disbelief.

"She likes men. But she likes men who're different. The oddballs. The unusuals. I'd be good as a hunchback, but I happen to know she's already had a hunchback. You, now, she's never met anything like you before."

"What do you mean?" Kil was half-angry.

"What I say. You're hard and tight—and different. Also, you've got something on your mind; she'll want to know what that is. If you take my advice you'll never tell her. She's the kind of woman that wouldn't like hearing about another woman."

"Oh, hell," said Kil, looking across at her. "I can't do this."

"She's your wire to the O.T.L.," said Dekko. "You want her, or don't you?"

Kil clenched his jaws together. The little muscles crawled in his cheek.

"All right," he said. He got up abruptly and began to walk across the room.

Melee Alain saw him coming. She lifted her eyes from the seated woman she was talking to and looked at him with a long, direct, and level glance. He came up to her.

"Hello, Meleé," he said.

She looked at him searchingly. Her head tilted back and her eyes widened slightly. They were green eyes flecked with little gold lights; they and the lips of her perfect mouth, parting a little, seemed to draw him almost physically to her. It was in that moment that Kil realized instantly and fully the danger of her. There is nothing so compelling as to be openly desired; and Meleé's desires were plain.

"Now don't tell me I've forgotten your name," she answered in a low voice. Her eyes invited him to join her in the polite fiction.

"Kil Bruner," he told her.

"Kil," she said. "Yes, Kil. How could it have slipped my mind—a strong name like that?" She put her hand lightly and firmly on his unsleeved arm. "Shall we go someplace where we can talk, Kil?"

"I'd like to."

She drew him across the room and through a little door into a small lounge.

"I reserved this," she said, closing the door carefully behind them. "It's not set for anyone else's Key." She led the way to a couch. "Sit down, Kil."

He seated himself beside her tentatively, feeling as large and awkward as a captive bear. For all her height, she moved with a casual suppleness; and now she leaned forward to a low table before them, pressing studs inset on its obsidian top.

"Drink?"

"Tequila," he said.

A section of the table top slid aside and the drinks rose up before them. She had chosen a tall mixed drink of some kind. She took it and leaned back into an angle of the couch, looking at him.

"You're quiet," she said.

He drank the tequilla all at once, bit into his slice of lemon and tossed it back into the dish. He scowled at it.

"This isn't going to work," he said; and started to stand up. She caught at his arm and held him back. He turned to look at her.

"You're a strange man," she said. She continued to hold him, staring into his eyes.

"Don't you want to make love to me?" she said, at last.

"Yes," he replied, truthfully enough. He was thinking that the fault was not in her attractiveness. The seductiveness of her burnt like a fierce flame in the closeness of the small, shaded lounge. The trouble lay in the fact that he was not a good liar—and he was having trouble believing what Dekko had told him about her.

"Then what is it?" When he still did not answer, she continued to study him. "You know, when I saw you coming across the floor to me, I felt something odd about you. But you seemed to be so full of purpose. I half-expected you to pick me up and carry me off right then. And now—you don't like this place, is that it?" she said with a sudden flash of intuition.

"It's not that," he said.

"You don't like me throwing myself at you, this way." She bit her lip, frowning. "Forgive me, Kil." Her face suddenly cleared and she drew her

legs up beneath her to sit curled in the angle of the
couch. The change was astonishing. It was as if
the fierce lamp of her beauty was suddenly
shaded, reduced to a soft and gentle glow. She
looked small and innocent, almost shy. "What
would you like, Kil?"

He looked squarely into her eyes. This, at least,
he could answer honestly.

"To see you again," he said.

"Away from all this, you mean?"

He nodded.

"I'm staying out at Bar Harbor. Do you know
where that is? Near Brainerd, Minnesota. It's a
resort area. I'm at a place called the Twin Pine
Lodge. You could come up for a few days."

"I will—" he hesitated. Now there was no
choice but to lie. "I'm tied up in a business deal
right now. That little man I was talking to before I
came up to you—"

"Oh," the monosyllable was dissapointed.
"Can't you put him off?"

"No, but if I could bring him along, for say a day
or two?"

She laughed, staring at him.

"There *can't* be anyone like you!" she said.

He shrugged, turning away.

"Well, then—"

"Oh, bring him, of course," she said. "You must
be some crazy, wild sort of efficiency expert. And
I must be infected with that same thing from contact with you. By all means place us both on your
schedule for the next few days." She moved suddenly over against him, all soft and warm and
appealing. "But kiss me, Kil."

He bent toward her lips; but the impalpable

presence of Ellen was suddenly between them. He stopped.

"No," he said, harshly.

Her face twisted suddenly as if she was going to cry.

"Oh, get out!" she cried, with something between a sob and a laugh. She pushed him away. "Get out of here—but come to me tomorrow at the Lodge."

He got up and went to the door. His hand was on it, when her voice stopped him.

"Kil!"

He turned to face her. She was looking at him with something on her face that was very like hatred.

"You'll kiss me," she said. "I'll make you kiss me."

He went out.

CHAPTER EIGHT

THE town of Brainerd was the terminal for the Bar Harbor resort area. Dekko and Kil took an airbus for the short hop there from Duluth, and a cab out to the resort area. Twin Pines Lodge, the cab's information service informed them, was a commercial resort with a capacity of about eighty people, situated on picturesque Gull Lake. It took them there.

They found themselves deposited before a wide stretch of lawn enclosed by an antique pole fence. Behind the fence, the lawn ran up a slope to a long lodge building on the crest of a low hill which hid the lake from them. Two large and symmetrical Norwegian pines flanking the Lodge's entrance explained the resort's name. A gateman halted them at the entrance in the pole fence to say that the resort's accommodations were already fully occupied. On Kil's mentioning Melee, however, he called up to the lodge building and turned again from his phone set to tell them that reservations for them had been made; but since the resort was crowded, he would have to put them in a single cabin. He took them in and guided them to a row of small cabins.

"Cabin eighteen," said the gateman.

He left them in it and departed. Kil had half expected to find Melee there and waiting for him. But she was nowhere to be seen. The small building was ordinary enough, equipped with its own food delivery system and the usual conveniences. They proceeded to settle down in it.

It was still early in the day. Dekko slipped out to look the situation over, and Kil found himself restless with time on his hands. He thought of going up to the lodge to look for Melee and decided against it. He stepped out and took the opposite direction, along past the cabins, toward the lake.

At the last cabin in the row, the door was opened and a deeply tanned, skinny man with a full gray-brown beard sat cross-legged on its threshold. He did not turn his head as Kil approached, but his eyes picked up the younger man and followed him until Kil was directly in front of him. Then:

"Good morning," he said, in a surprisingly bass voice.

Kil stopped.

"Hello," he answered, a little uncertainly.

"That's a very interesting Key band." There was

humor in the bright eyes above the beard. "Almost the duplicate of my own."

"What—" Kil frowned, then suddenly understood. He reached out his wrist and the seated man lifted his own Key to touch it to Kil's. There was a tingle that ran suddenly around Kil's skin under the band.

"As I thought," said the seated man. "Sit down, won't you? I'm Anton Bolievsky. And not at all as eccentric as I look, by the way. Won't you sit down?"

Kil looked around him. There was a leveled off tree stump near the doorway to which a cushioned top had been fixed. Kil seated himself on this.

"Thanks," he said.

"Don't thank me," replied Anton Bolievsky. "I've been hoping you'd come by this way ever since I saw you get here. You're an unusual sort of man to run into here. Mind if I ask your name?"

"Oh, sorry," said Kil. "Kil Bruner."

"Kil—Bruner." Bolievsky nodded thoughtfully. "I'll remember that."

Kil looked at him curiously.

"You're a member of the Thieves Guild?" he asked.

"Kil," said the other. "I'm everything. Doctor, lawyer, Indian Chief; you've met our friend Toy, of course?"

"Yes." Kil nodded

"Well, there you have it. Toy represents the emotional failure of our age. I represent the intellectual failure. Master of all trades and a good, honest jack at none of them." He cocked his head at Kil. "You don't believe me?"

"Well, I—" Kil found himself feeling a sudden curious attraction to this man. The directness of him raised a sympathetic vibration in the metal of Kil's own direct self. "What do you mean, he represents emotional failure?"

Bolievsky smiled in his beard.

"He's one of the mythological characters of our modern fairy-tale. The giant Apathy, ruler of the kingdom of I Give Up. Toy has gone hunting for dragons without finding any. And since he can't be St. George, he won't play. We've got other failures in that line, but Toy's far and away the most spectacular of them."

"I suppose he can't help it," said Kil, thoughtfully, "being born twice as big as anyone else and so forth."

"Don't you ever think it," Bolievsky shook his head. "That's just his excuse. He doesn't *want* to help it—and that's a major sin in anyone, not wanting something enough. Our most common fault nowadays. We want this, we want that, but not hard enough to go out and get it. We want a world without Files prodding us from spot to spot, but not enough to really get down to work and do something about it. And meanwhile the people who want something or other selfishly, for themselves, and want it hard enough, go out and get it just because of the type of attitude that Toy personifies."

Kil found himself smiling for the first time since Ellen had disappeared.

"And you're an exception?" he said.

"Oh—" Bolievsky smiled wryly. "I'm much more deeply damned. As I say, I'm an intellectual failure. In-tel-lec-tu-al fail-ure." He rolled the words out. "I don't know what I want. I have yet to decide on a career, which is somewhat startling when you stop to consider that I'm now sixty-three years old. I have an excellent mind and a great deal of energy. My health is good and I eat like a horse. I have a doctorate in philosophy and degrees in history, economics, chemistry, physics, psychology and biology. I have read widely in other fields, and speak and read—or at least read—twelve dead languages. I have dabbled in mysticism, ancient religions, politics, yoga; in short, in everything animal, vegetable and mineral. I am the very model of a modern intellectual. Will you believe me," said Bolievsky, earnestly, reaching out and laying a long, thin hand on Kil's knee, "when I tell you that I sometimes wonder about the purpose for which I was put into this world?"

"No," said Kil. "But why tell me all this?"

"Because you have a strange air about you. As if you might possibly be one of those rare human animals who does know what he wants. Do you?"

Kil laughed.

"And what if I did?"

"Why then," said Bolievsky, letting his hand drop from Kil's knee and drawing himself up stiffly, "you're the most likely candidate for Superman. Laugh if you like. Listen!" He held up one finger. "Once upon a time when Man was galloping about in a bearskin, hitting small animals over the head with a club and climbing trees to get away from the big ones; drying in the sun, soaking in the rain, and freezing in the snow and wind, and all the time wondering where his next meal was coming from, he sat down and made a list of his wants. Here—'' Bolievsky reached back around and inside the doorway, and came out with a pen and a pad of paper. "Like this.''

He wrote rapidly. When he was finished, he handed the sheet to Kil. Kil looked at it. On it was a list, with the title:

LIST OF NEEDS AND WANTS
by Ima Caveman

Something to kill large animals
Something to kill bad enemies
A bearskin that doesn't wear out
A cave that is (a) warm when it's cold out
                (b) cool when it's hot out
Something to take care of evil spirits
Something to fix me when I'm hurt or sick
All the food and drink I'll ever need
Something to make people good
Something just in case they are bad anyway

Kil laughed again, and handed the sheet back. "What about it?'' he asked.

"Just this,'' said Bolievsky, and wrote again, on the same page. So that now it read:

LIST OF NEEDS
AND WANTS   by Ima Caveman

Something to kill large animals	weapons
Something to kill bad enemies	nuclear weapons
A bearskin that doesn't wear out	plastic clothing
A cave that is (a) warm when it's cold out (b) cool when it's hot out	heating and air conditioning
Something to take care of evil spirits	education
Something to fix me when I'm hurt or sick	modern medicine
All the food and drink I'll ever need	modern production methods
Something to make people good	religion
Something just in case they are bad anyway	organized society

He handed it back to Kil. Kil read it.

"You see," said Bolievsky. "We present-day, dressed-up cavemen have answered our full list of wants. Now we have answered it. The day of the caveman's millennium is at hand. Or should be. What do you think?"

"I think," said Kil, dryly, "that maybe we aren't cavemen any longer."

"Exactly!" cried Bolievsky. "By satisfying the caveman, we have destroyed him. He was nothing more than a bundle of wants to start off with. Enter the Superman—the successor to the caveman, who has discovered a new want. Now," he said, peering at Kil, "perhaps a superman like yourself would condescend to tell an old destroyed caveman like *myself* what that want might be?"

Kil smiled, shook his head and handed the sheet back. He got up from the stump.

"I haven't got the slightest idea," he said. "But if I think of something, I'll let you know."

"Yes—" said Bolievsky, in a disappointed tone, gnawing at his beard and staring at the paper in his hand.

Kil turned and walked off.

He went back to the cabin he shared with Dekko, doing a little thinking himself as he went.

Several hours later, Dekko showed up. He came in quietly, shut the cabin door behind him, and from his pocket produced a small instrument not much larger than the Key on his wrist. With this he made a tour of all three rooms without speaking. When he was finished he came back to Kil, who had been watching him from the couch where he had been sitting and reading.

"All right," said Dekko, sitting down. "This is it."

Kil laid his scanner aside.

"This is what?" he asked.

"This place. The O.T.L. It's all O.T.L.: a semi-permanent set-up. They rotate people like Stick headquarters. Everybody here is a representative from some Society, or Group, or Organization.

And by the way, I think your girl friend knows we're up to something."

"My girl friend?"

"Melee."

"What the hell do you mean?" snapped Kil. "You were the one that thought up the idea of getting acquainted with her in the first place."

Dekko took time out to grin.

"Sure. *Her*, then. Anyway, I could be wrong about her suspecting, too. Well, it doesn't matter. I still think we can make out all right. There'll be something doing at the Lodge tonight, and we're going to listen in on it. Then we'll figure out where to go from there. It'll mean taking a few chances, though." He looked questioningly at Kil.

"Whatever's necessary," said Kil, grimly.

"Good, then. We've got to wait until dark. Catch a nap if you can."

Dekko walked into his own bedroom and dropped on the bed there. Two minutes later, when Kil passed the doorway on the way to his own room, the smaller man was already heavily and silently asleep.

Kil awoke to find Dekko shaking him. He sat up, dull-witted with sleep. The window of his room was a square of darkness and Dekko himself was a dim, indistinct figure bending over him.

"No lights," said Dekko. "Come on."

Kil sat up, swung his legs over the edge of the bed and sat there, scrubbing some life back into his sleepy face. Partially recovered after a moment, he pushed himself to his feet and lurched out of his room, down the short hall and into the cabin's living room, dusky in deep shadow from the thin fringe of dying daylight in the western sky.

Dekko was sitting at a low table, working with small things in the darkness, either by virtue of cat-like eyesight or just plain feel; it was not clear to Kil which. After a while he finished, gathered them up and stood up himself.

"All right," he said. "We're set. Come on."

He led the way out of the door into the night that had now fallen. Slowly, in the darkness, they moved uphill and shortly they came up close under a set of large, one-way windows, now opaqued, in the west wing of the lodge.

"Wait here," said Dekko. He moved up about five feet to a corner of one of the windows. There was a soft, almost inaudible sighing sound, and a pin-prick of light appeared in the darkness of the opaqued window. Dekko backed off towards Kil, knelt down and drove a short, thin, black rod into the earth, in line with the window.

"Now," he said.

Dekko leading, they moved back into the cover of a small clump of pine.

"Down," said Dekko.

They went down on their stomachs on the hard turf and Dekko set up before them a small box on tripod legs. He plugged two cords into the box, cords which terminated in hooded spectacles, each with a small button attached to the right temple.

"Button in your ear," whispered Dekko, slipping his pair of the spectacles on. Kil followed suit and found himself suddenly plunged into the most absolute darkness. Fiddling with the frame of the spectacles, he discovered a small lever; and this, when he shifted it, unopaqued the lenses before him so that normal vision of the night came back to him.

"Now here," whispered Dekko, "is the doby prize. Four hundred alone, this little looper cost you."

Very gently, he produced a cube-shape no larger than a ring box. Gently, he opened it. By the illumination of some fluorescent pigment in the walls of the box, Kil saw what seemed to be a sleeping fly with a band of dull black about its thorax.

"Special resistant strain," said Dekko. "This area will have been sprayed, but the looper should be good for about an hour. Now we check—"

His fingers moved over the box on the three tripod legs. The band of dull black on the fly seemed to glitter briefly with obsidian lights. And the fly stirred. With insect drowsiness it fluttered its wings, cleaned its forelegs and abruptly took off, disappearing in the dark.

Dekko gestured with one finger to the spectacles and Kil, reaching up, moved the little built-in lever to his original position. Abruptly, his mind reeled with something like vertigo as his perceptions told him he was weaving through the night air some two feet or so above the ground. The dark mass of the Lodge loomed up over him. The pin-prick of light attracted and he flew toward it.

The hole in the window grew as he approached. He flew to it, clung to the pane below it, and squeezed through into brilliance. He found himself only inches above the floor in a large room filled with a long conference table at which people sat. Soundlessly, he flew up and clung to the

ceiling. The scene reeled, what was up now be-
coming down; and Kil found himself gazing
down at the heads of those at the table.

The group seated about did not fill the table.
There was space for perhaps as many more again.
Those that were there, therefore, were clustered
around one end at which sat a slim, brown-
headed young man with a striking resemblance to
Melee.

"—as of the twenty-third," this young man was
saying. "I don't like this looseness in the organization. Rumor of Sub-E has leaked to the Unstabs and whoever leaked it was from one of our
inner group of Societies."

"Question," said a short man with a hard,
round face above a grey tunic. "You're sure of
that?"

"The original mention of Sub-E was in the report of a junior codist of the World Police, who
received a reference to it from Files while coding
for a solution on a series of unexplained, super-
natural sort of phenomena which has been coming to Police notice during the last few years. He
did not check back immediately, for some reason
and when he did, all information on Sub-E, in-
cluding the name itself, had become unavailable
under the self-censoring circuit. His report was
copied by one of our agents inside the Police and
handed directly to me."

"I'd say the responsibility might be yours," said
the hard-faced man.

"No you wouldn't," replied the young man
pleasantly. "No you wouldn't, Polano, at all."

There was no change of expression either in his

voice or his face, but a slight pause followed his words, and the hard-faced man said no more.

"The agent?" suggested somebody else.

"Perfectly trustworthy," answered the young man, turning his attention to this new speaker. "Not conditioned, unfortunately, since he's liable to regular check as Police Personnel. But I had a cover made on his movements and he didn't have any chance at all to pass off the information, up until the time I mentioned it to a meeting of this council, six months ago."

"Question?" said a dark-skinned woman sitting farther down the table. "What is this self-censoring circuit business? It's the first I've heard of any such thing."

"Police-restricted information," said the young man, smiling at her. "As far as we can gather, it seems to be some sort of ultimate control system whereby Files can censor itself in the case of information which it computes as having a high probability index of danger to the public welfare."

"Isn't there someone in the Police who can throw out the censoring circuit and get the information?"

The young man shrugged.

"You know—" he said. "The Police have always insisted that even they don't know where Files is located. As far as the men we've got in their ranks can tell, they're telling the truth. We know that the leads from the coding machines go to a central cable which drops directly down, vertically into the ground, for fifteen hundred feet before it goes through a completely spy-proof shield and we lose it completely. Where it comes up, and if it comes up, is anybody's guess."

"We ought to be able to find out somehow," murmured a tall, thin man further up the table.

"We're working on it." The young man leaned forward a little over the table. "None of you should forget that while we've got some sympathizers and adherents among the Police, we're a long way from being in possession of all their top men and all their top secrets, by a long shot. For one thing, the Commissioner continues to slip through our fingers."

"The Commissioner!" It was the hard-faced man again. "Are you even sure there is such a man?"

"Perfectly sure," replied the young man, coolly. "He handles all the long range policy planning and has authority even over the official six-months heads when each one is in office. But outside of that fact and the scrap information that he's known to the Police themselves as McElroy—"

—Out on the hillside, under the stars, Kil started so hard that the spectacles almost slipped off his nose—

"—we don't know anything about him. Except, of course, that he's a fantastically capable man."

"Too capable for you to handle, maybe," said the hard-faced man, "by yourself this way. If—"

"No, Polano," said the young man, gently. "Just because I give credit where credit is due, don't jump to a false conclusion. You all know my capabilities, I think. And none of you doubt them, do you?" His glance covered the table, from which there was silence. "What I was saying was just that this McElroy is a capable opponent. In fact—" his smile broadening, the young man tilted back his head and looked up at the ceiling where the fly was. To Kil, it seemed as if his eyes were staring directly into Kil's own. "In fact," the young man repeated, "he may be the very person who's spying upon us at this moment. *Take him, men!*"

Warned too late, Kil ripped frantically at his spectacles. But they were hardly halfway off before two heavy bodies landed simultaneously upon him. Fighting furiously, he was conscious of something tremendously hard that collided with his head and then nothing.

CHAPTER NINE

Kɪʟ came back, to light, and warmth and consciousness. The bright glare of a well-lit room dazzled his eyes and his head was aching furiously. Even as he awoke, however, this last faded and disappeared, leaving only a dull, uncomfortable feeling, as if the ache had not so much been done away with, as tucked away in the back of his mind somewhere and hidden from conscious discovery by his nerves.

"That should do it," said a voice; and Kil, looksmall, square, comfortable room. The young man who so resembled Melee, speaking. He was putting aside on a table a small atomizer half-full of colorless liquid. "How do you feel now?"

"Better," muttered Kil.

He looked around him. He was in the same conference room he had been watching, but only a few of the people he had seen through the medium of the fly were there. Among these was Melee, who had not earlier been present at the conference. She regarded him from a little distance, with no readable expression.

"Where's Dekko?" asked Kil, thickly.

"Your friend?" said the young man. "He seems to have got away—for the moment, anyway. We ought to have him in an hour or so." He looked at Kil, humorously. "You're something new even among Melee's boy friends. What did you expect to gain by spying on her?"

Kil, about to retort in astonishment, caught a particular intensity in the young man's gaze and checked himself in time from reacting.

"Well," went on the young man. "Since this is a family matter, I think maybe the three of us would be better off talking it over in private. So if you'll come with me, Melee, and," he turned to Kil again, "you too, we'll go to my study."

Kil got somewhat shakily to his feet and followed brother and sister out of the room.

They went down a short hallway and into a small, square, comfortable room. The young man closed the door behind them and made some adjustments in a small, clock-like mechanism attached to it.

"There," he said, coming further into the room and throwing himself loosely into a chair. "Sit down, Melee. You too, Kil. Oh, by the way, Kil, Mali is my name. As you've probably guessed, Melee and I are twins. Now, let's get down to the truth of this. Just what were you after?"

"Kil!" said Melee, suddenly.

"Hush now, baby," interrupted Mali, gently, "let him tell me."

"I want to find my wife," said Kil, bluntly.

Melee's face suddenly went pale; and Mali's eyebrows went up.

Kil told him, fully and honestly. After he had finished, Mali stared at him for a long moment in silence and then turned to his sister.

"Well," he said. "What do you think of this? Or did you know it before?"

With a sudden furious movement, she whipped her head away from him, and stood staring into a far corner of the room, without answering.

"Now," he said, in that same gentle tone, "I wasn't criticising. You shouldn't fight me, baby. Come here."

He held out his hand. Slowly she looked back at him. Slowly she walked over to his chair and he took her lightly by the wrist.

"My sister," he said, softly, turning to Kil, "is very insecure. She needs constant reassurance."

Seeing her as she stood there, nakedly docile, Kil suddenly realized the terrible quality of truth in Mali's words. And Dekko's assessment: "She got tangle circuits up top," came back to him.

"She doesn't believe anyone—even me sometimes. But she should," went on Mali, tenderly. "I've looked out for her since she was a little girl, haven't I, Melee?"

"Yes," she murmured, almost inaudibly, her face downcast toward the carpet and looking at neither one of them.

"Ever since our father died; and we were children. I've never let anyone hurt you, have I, Melee?"

She shook her head, still staring at the carpet.

"No," she whispered.

"You know you can trust me, then, don't you?"

She nodded.

"Then you let me handle this in my own way." He let go of her wrist and sat looking at her. "Go back and sit down, baby. I'll take care of everything."

She walked away to a distant chair and sat down apart. He turned back to Kil.

"I don't know if I believe you or not," he said. "But it's easy enough to check your story. I can check quite simply with the Acapulco local police, Marsk, and the Ace you say you talked to. This Dekko—we should have him shortly. As far as McElroy's concerned—" he paused and looked at Kil, for a long, calculating moment. "Well, we'll see if your story checks."

"And if it checks," demanded Kil, "what?"

"Why I'll decide whether you're telling the truth or not. And if you are, I might help you."

"You?"

"I. The O.T.L. That's what you say you were after here, wasn't it? Help from the O.T.L. to find your wife?"

"Can you speak for the whole O.T.L.?" said Kil, bluntly.

Mali smiled.

"Yes," he said. "Yes, we have a little convention here. We pretend that I'm just one of a governing board for handling the O.T.L. and the member societies as a unit. But it's just that—a convention."

Kil considered him, grimly and a little skeptically.

"You think a lot of yourself."

"That's right," replied Mali, evenly. "I do."

Kil shrugged and went back to the main topic.

"You said you might help me. If you do, what kind of price do you charge?"

"That'd depend." Mali looked at him. "It might be we'd want you to join us."

"Join you?"

Mali nodded. His eyes and face gave absolutely no clue to whether he was serious or not.

"You said you were a mnemonic engineer somewhere in that story of yours," he said. "Because mnemonic engineers are necessarily Class A's, we seldom get one in a Society."

Kil scowled at him.

"I thought this O.T.L. of yours was an organization of the heads of other Societies, only."

"Who told you that?" countered Mali.

"I just heard it."

"Then you heard only part of the truth. There's more to it than that."

Kil abandoned his curiosity in that direction.

"What about—you haven't told me how you might be able to find my wife," he said.

"Well," answered Mali, "we'd do pretty much what your Ace said he could do, only we'd do it more efficiently and with a great many more people. The Societies are a fine instrument in the right hands. I could have more than two million people keeping their eyes open for your wife inside of twenty-four hours. Maybe fifty million in the long run."

"And I'd pay you for that by joining this outfit of yours?"

Mali nodded.

"Just what would that mean?"

"Not a lot," answered Mali. "We'd merely want to be sure of you and your loyalty, which in this case would mean you'd be examined under hypnosis to definitely establish the facts about you for your dossier. And at the same time you'd be given loyalty conditioning."

"I'm not sure I like that second."

Mali shrugged.

"We're like any other outfit today. I don't suppose you've objected to hypno conditioning when you were working on something involving a trade secret of one company or another."

Kil frowned.

"That's not the same thing."

"Well—" Mali got to his feet. "Think it over. Melee will show you a room in the Lodge here when you can stay for the rest of the night. Consider yourself under something like house arrest until we find out about you."

Kil rose also.

"I'd like to know just how much truth there is in what you say," he said.

Mali smiled.

"A lot of people say that to me." He nodded. "Good night," he said and went out the door.

Kil stood staring after him. The voice of Melee at his elbow made him turn.

"This way, Kil."

He followed her out by another door. Down a somewhat longer hallway, this time, they came upon a moving ramp rising to the second story of the lodge. She led the way up this and along the corridor above to a door which she opened with her Key.

"Here," she said.

She stood aside to let him enter, then followed him in, closing the door behind her. Kil found himself in a comfortable bedroom, a little larger than its equivalent would have been in an overnight Class A hotel, and somewhat more luxuriously furnished. He turned about to Melee and found her close to him, so close indeed that her breasts brushed against him as he turned.

"Well—thanks," he said. "I'll see you in the morning, I suppose."

She looked up into his face.

"Kil," she said, uncertainly. "Kil, offer me a drink, or something, will you? Don't make me go just yet."

"A drink?" He swung about and saw the transparent door of a liquor cabinet, recessed in one wall. "Oh well, what would you like?"

He went across to the cabinet. To his secret relief, instead of following him, she crossed the room in the opposite direction and sank down on a couch.

"A little cognac," she said. "Have one with me, Kil."

"All right." He answered with his back still toward her.

He opened the cabinet, selected a pair of glasses and splashed a little of the amber cognac into each of them. He closed the cabinet door and carried the glasses back across the room.

"Here you are," he said, sitting down in a chair opposite her. She accepted the glass from him, holding it in slim fingers. Abruptly, she shuddered and drank quickly, emptying it almost at once.

"Please, Kil," she said, holding it out at arm's length. "Another."

Kil scowled, but took the glass and getting up, went back to the cabinet for a refill. He brought it to her and she looked up at him as she accepted it, almost abjectly.

"Don't look so angry, please," she said. "Talk to me, Kil. Say something."

"Talk—about what?" he asked.

"Tell me about your wife. What does she look like, Kil?"

He rubbed his nose.

"Well, she's small," he said. "She's got blonde hair. And blue eyes. And a soft voice."

"Is she pretty?" A momentary shadow passed across Melee's eyes. "Much prettier than I am?"

Kil shook his head, looking at her.

"No," he said, slowly, "you know she wouldn't be."

"I don't," she answered, staring not at him, but away across the room. "No, I don't. I never do. How would I know?" Her hands twisted on the glass. "There's millions of women in the world—maybe all of them prettier than I am." And she shuddered again.

"Drink the cognac," said Kil, a little more softly. Her eyes came gratefully around to focus on him.

"Drink with me, Kil." She extended her glass and, a little self-consciously, he touched it with his own. And then, seeing that she once more intended to gulp all her drink at once, he tossed all of his own down. It burned fiercely in his throat and gullet.

"There," he said. "Now—" Abruptly, a tremor passed through him and the room seemed to cant suddenly to one side. A wave of dizziness, but somehow different, rippled his vision, and through its distortion, as the carpeted floor came swooping up to meet him, he could just see Melee. She was setting down her glass and watching him, with her lips just beginning to curve, as he fell, into a smile.

CHAPTER TEN

KIL came to the realization that he had been awake for some time, staring without seeing the beamed ceiling above him. Shifting himself slowly to the edge of the bed, he sat unclothed, examining himself and the room to which Melee had brought him—yes, it must have been the night before, for now the bright sunlight, streaming in at an angle which indicated morning, lit up his undressed condition and the rumpled state of the bed. There was sweat on his forehead and a clutching, all-obsessive feeling that something was terribly wrong. *What had happened?* But nothing came to him, only the empty, scooped-out feeling of something drastic that had taken place. He jumped to his feet and took three quick strides to stand in front of a mirror across the room. His own image looked back at him as lean and uncompromising as ever. Foolishly, he felt his arms and legs and the nerves in them reacted to his fingers' pressure in honest fashion. His body reported all well. Only a slight soreness behind one ear, where he might have hit his head in falling after he was drugged, and a slight headache, lopsided in that area, interrupted the general sense of physical well-being. But he felt hollow inside.

He walked over to a closet set in the wall and, opening it, found clothes—the ones he had worn the night before as well as several plastic throwaway outfits that looked to be his size. Out of automatic instincts and habits of cleanliness, he reached for one of these latter, but an odd repugnance made him draw his hand back and he dressed instead in his tunic and kilt of the previous day.

Dressed, he tried his door and found it unlocked. He stepped through it and out into the corridor. Some thirty feet along this corridor, he came on a door ajar, about where he remembered the study to have been. He went in.

It was not the study after all, but a larger room, a lounge of some sort with a wall-wide window beside which sat a breakfast table as yet uncleared. Melee stood by the table, looking out at the trees and the grounds of the lakeward side of the resort. From this height, the blue windings of the lake could be seen beyond the tops of the trees. A small breeze blew from it, through the wall-window, which had been rolled back, and the soft, clean air of morning came to Kil's nostrils.

At the sight of her, standing with her back to him, a deep feeling of desire stirred unexpectedly in Kil and he went forward until he stood at her side.

"Morning," he said.

She turned slowly to face him. On her lips was an echo of the triumphant smile of the night before, but it faded as she regarded him, changing into something eager and half-fearful.

"Kiss me," she said.

Kil put his arms around her and drew her to him. He kissed her, feeling the hot coal of desire that was new within him burst suddenly into blazing heat. Abruptly, she wrenched away from him.

"Damn you!" she cried. "Oh, damn you!"

Her fists were clenched and her face was screwed up in pain. When he moved toward her again, she evaded him.

"What is this?" demanded Kil, sharply.

"It's not you!" She beat with her fists on the back of a chair. "It's not you! I thought I wouldn't mind, but I do. I do!"

"What do you mean?"

She faced him.

"I said I'd make you kiss me." Her eyes glittered with tears. "And I have. But now I don't want it that way—that way—"

"What way?" said Kil, staring at her.

"Via," said a soft voice behind him, "the hypno route."

Kil turned to see Mali standing in an open doorway leading to an adjoining room, a scanner in his hand. As Kil watched, Mali came all the way into the room, shutting the door behind him. He put down the reel on a coffee table and pressed a button. The other door closed and the window slid noiselessly back into position, sealing the room.

"Melee jumped the gun," said Mali, coming up

to him. In the bright morning light, the head of the
O.T.L. looked young and diffident, like a polite
schoolboy. "She didn't wait for the checks on
your story to come through. They have now, by
the way. You're quite a truthful man. But as I say,
she saw to it that you were conditioned last
night." He turned to look at Melee, but she stayed
rigid, her back to both men.

"Conditioned!" said Kil.

"Yes, and there's something strange about it,
too," continued Mali, in the same casual tone
from which his voice never varied. Almost, he
could have been discussing the weather planned
that week for the district. "You took the com-
mands readily enough. You've probably noticed
that your reactions toward Melee are considerably
greater now than any you may have toward your
wife. Or any other woman for that matter. And
you'll also discover a comparable loyalty to the
O.T.L. as a group and to me, myself, as an individual. But the search didn't work out at all well."

"The *search!*"

Kil felt the cold fingers of horror crawling down
his spine. Hypnotic search was a highly tricky,
rigidly restricted psychiatric technique used on
the dangerously disturbed Unstab, or proved vio-
lator of the world peace. "You had the guts to
—illegally—and you *tell* me about it!"

"It's quite safe," replied Mail, with a gentle
wave of his hand. "Your loyalty won't permit you
to give me away. Will it?" He smiled; and Kil,
feeling the emotions surging within him, discovered that this was only too true. "I can talk as
freely in front of you as I could in front of—a dog,
say. Though that's putting it a little harshly."

Kil stared at him, realizing with an empty horror that he could not even hate the man.

"Yes," said Mali, reaching for a bunch of grapes that still lay in the fruit bowl in the center of the breakfast table. "But to get back to the subject— want a grape? No? The search uncovered nothing; just as if there had been nothing to uncover. And I know differently: Don't I? Does your new loyalty have any suggestions that might help me with this problem?"

"I don't know what you're talking about," said Kil, numbly. He sat down heavily. Mali gazed at him, curiously.

"To a certain extent, that's probably correct," he said, agreeably, eating grapes one by one from the bunch. "You fill a rather odd position, Kil, whether you know it or not. For some reason—by some accident or design—you've become the focal point of our struggle at the present moment."

"What struggle?"

"What struggle?" repeated Mali. "Why, the same struggle that's been going on since the world began: to see who's going to be the one to control things. There's at least two—and I think three—of us busy at it right now. And you're in the middle. It's sort of as if you were a chess piece being manipulated in turn by three opposing players, all of them hidden from each other. We all try to figure out from what you do just who it was made you do it, and what his reasons were for exactly that move."

Kil shook his head disbelievingly.

"Oh, yes," said Mali. "Yes indeed, Kil. The two most important men in the world today are McElroy and myself. It wasn't just chance that led you first to him and then to me. It couldn't be. I'm the most powerful individual on Earth and McElroy is the—most elusive, certainly. Yet you trot from him to me with no more difficulty than going from one store to another. How did you manage that? Can you tell me?"

Kil felt the compulsion on him to answer.

"Dekko," he said reluctantly.

"Hmm," said Mali, holding the grapes forgotten in one hand, "as far as that goes, I'm pretty sure that Dekko of yours belongs to McElroy. He's another mystery. But a minor one. You're the big one, you and—" he broke off suddenly, staring out the window. After a moment, he turned back to Kil.

"What do you know about The Project?" he demanded. "And Sub-E?"

Kil lifted his head in amazement.

"Nothing," he said.

"And yet," said Mali, looking at him closely, "your wife's certainly a member and knows all about it."

Kil felt a sudden small stir of excitement in him.

"A member? What—?" he said.

"Exactly. What?" Mali leaned toward him, his eyes oddly compelling. "The Project's an organization that has something called Sub-E. And Sub-E is maybe the secret of their ability to do things that are physically impossible, like hiding from myself and the Police, on this Earth where there's no place to hide. Does that jog your memory? Answer me!"

"Don't the Police know?"

"No. The Police do not know. Any more than I

know. And I have to know. I could crush the
Police like that, tomorrow, Kil," and Mali closed
his hand before Kil's face, "and they know it. But
they know I don't dare try it as long as this question mark exists, this other power that may have a
weapon on its Sub-E that I can't match. Now answer me, does this, all this, make you remember
anything?"

"No," said Kil.

Mali drew a deep breath and straightened up.
His eyes went away from Kil and focused on the
middle distance as his attention turned inward.
Kil saw a valuable moment slipping away from
him.

"I don't believe you," he said.

Mali's attention came back with a jerk.

"Don't believe what?" he said.

"What you said about being able to crush the
Police."

Mali smiled at him. He became conscious of the
grapes still in his hand and threw them down on
the table.

"There's only six million of them, Kil," he said.
"And the world is sick of them, and Files, and a
Key on every wrist. Your little group of A. Stabs
are the exception, and there's nothing wonderful
in that. Under almost any system there's bound to
be found some people who are suited to it. What it
boils down to is we've been living in a temporary
state of emergency for a hundred years. The wonder is that it hasn't cracked before now."

"War!" said Kil. He pronounced the word with
the deep, almost instinctive intonation of shock
and horror typical in a man of his time.

"No such thing," replied Mali, swiftly. "Skirmishes, maybe, but only to help along the shift in balance of power. The organized Societies are inevitably bound to follow a situation of Police control and supplant it."

"Why?"

"Because," said Mali, quite earnestly, "they offer man what Files has taken away from him: a social structure, a solid social structure to build his own life inside."

Kil shook his head, not knowing exactly why he was disagreeing, but disagreeing reflexively.

"Believe me," said Mali, looking at him. "Files was a mistake. They thought then that man couldn't go on living and developing with the threat of atomic annihilation constantly hanging over him. They forgot that men have built on the sides of a volcano before. More important than the volcano is the building. We all need it— something solid to tie to—a place to lie down. And that's what none of us have now, under Files and the Police, all four billions of us, wanderers over the face of the globe."

For a moment, Mali's easy going voice rang with a true note of idealism.

"So that's why you do these things?" said Kil.

Mali laughed and slipped back into his customary manner.

"No," he said. "In my case, conviction followed conversion. No, Kil, you probably think I've got delusions of grandeur, a Napoleon, an Alexander complex. It's a lot more prosaic than that. I just happen to be capable and started out wanting little things. Then as I got those, I wanted bigger and bigger things, more and more, until now. . . ."

"Until now you want the world."

"Why not?" asked Mali.

Kil shook his head, again, stubbornly.

"Why not just ignore the Project?" he said.

"Because," answered Mali, quietly, "they seem to be capable of doing all sorts of impossible things; and not the least of these is the fact that they seem to be already free of Files. They don't wear Keys—" he checked himself suddenly, his eyes pouncing on Kil. "What is it?"

"Nothing," said Kil, hastily.

"Must I appeal to your new sense of loyalty for an answer?"

"The—" the words struggled from Kil's throat, "the old man had no Key."

"The old man who took your wife off with him?" Mali considered Kil, no longer smiling. "Now why, I wonder, didn't that come out under the Search. The Project may have—" He let the words trail off. Abruptly, he turned.

"Keep thinking, Kil," he said. "Somewhere in you there's enough information buried in five years of association with your wife to tell us where the Project hides itself. We'll get it eventually. If you think of anything more that might be useful to me, come and find me. Meanwhile, stay on the grounds."

He walked out through the door, and was gone.

Kil stared after him for a short moment; and then turned to Melee. She had also turned and was facing him with one of her strange unreadable expressions.

"Let's go for a walk," she said. "Come on, Kil. "We'll go down by the lake and get away from this place and everything."

He nodded, scarcely listening. His mind was whirling with thoughts of Ellen and the old man who had worn no Key on his wrist.

Almost in a daze, he followed Melee, as she once more opened the window and stepped through it to the turf below. Side by side and saying nothing, they cut across to the gravel path slanting downhill from the lodge, and followed it around its curve past the row of cabins.

They passed the cabin in which Kil and Dekko had been lodged the day before. The ghost of that yesterday seemed more than twenty-four hours old as Kil looked at it. Almost it seemed as if it might have been weeks back that he and Dekko had rested here, waiting for night so that they could go up to spy on the Lodge. Thinking of the little man reminded Kil.

"What happened to Dekko?" he asked Melee.

"He hasn't been caught yet," she answered absently, walking along with her eyes fixed on the path. A momentary concern and sympathy for the slight hunchback stirred briefly in Kil's mind and was drowned immediately by his conditioning.

They passed the other cabins and drew level with the one that housed Anton Bolievsky. As before, the old man that looked so young was sitting cross-legged in the doorway.

"Good morning," he said, as they came up. Kil stopped. Melee continued on as if she had not heard.

"Hello," said Kil.

They looked at each other.

"Your particular aura of purposefulness," said Anton, "seems dimmed, but not extinguished. You are a very fortunate young man."

"What do you mean?" asked Kil.

"Merely trying to put into words a feeling I get," replied the other. "You remember our talk yesterday?"

"Of course."

"It made me think. Did it make you think?"

"Kil!" called Melee, impatiently, from the bend in path where it headed into the belt of trees that hid the lake.

"I—I've got to go," said Kil. "Maybe we can get together for a talk, later."

"Yes," said Anton.

Kil turned and hurried off, wondering at himself. Melee had already gone on again down the path and disappeared into the woods. He hurried ahead, caught a glimpse of her silver tunic through the green branches, and increased his pace. The path wound about, now that it was among the trees, and she was nowhere to be seen. Twenty yards further on, however, he came suddenly around a sharp turn and literally ran into her. She was standing with her back to him, staring out over the lake; but as they collided, she turned swiftly and clung to him. And he saw with astonishment that she was crying, silently and fiercely.

"Melee—" he said.

"Oh, Kil," she moaned. "Why do I do these things? Why?"

But then her words were lost to him; for, even as he put his arms instinctively around her, he looked over her shoulder and saw the full expanse of the lake. One of the larger bodies of water in the area, it sparkled as the sun picked highlights among its ripples. And as it had been before, when he looked out McElroy's window on Lake Superior, and when he came up from the meeting place of the Panthers and faced the Pacific, the world weaved around him. The deep and crying need for Ellen, only Ellen, rose irresistibly within him. Stronger . . . stronger . . . stronger by far than the time before, which had been stronger than the first time, stronger than any hpynotic condition that ever had been or could be, it called him. Ellen . . . Ellen . . . Ellen. . . .

Dimly he was conscious of a flash of silver tunic before his eyes and a woman's scream. And then he was free and running, running, running. . . .

CHAPTER ELEVEN

THE first few hours were blurred. After that, when he at last came fully to himself again, he was riding down an ancient highway in an all-purpose bug, its squashy flotons humming merrily as it buzzed along at somewhere around a hundred and ten kilometers an hour. The driver was a wiry old botanical technician whose love for his bug was unbounded and voluble.

"I've carted her all over the world with me. Trade her in, says the home office. Trade, hell, I told them. I got nothing else that belongs to me, on the go all the time. Hortense, she's mine. I had her in India and up and down the Andes in South A. Up and down the Sierra Madres, too, That wasn't bad. It's timber that stops you. Trees so thick you can't see through—going to Duluth, you said?"

"What? Oh—. Yes. . . ." said Kil.

"Thought that's what you said. My folks come

from Duluth, originally. Well, not Duluth proper—around Two Harbors. Of course I don't remember it myself, but I recall my grandfather telling me about how the lamprey's came in there and spoiled the fishing, just about cleaned out all the lake trout. Ever see a picture of a lamprey? The way he described them—"

Kil leaned back against the foam cushions of the bug, letting the words flow around him and nodding whenever it seemed expedient. His mind felt exhausted, drained of feeling. He tried to force it to concentrate on his situation, to think about the future, but the effort was beyond him at the moment. He gave up, rocking with the cab of the bug and half-listening.

"—world going to hell. Just another old crank talking, you'll probably say. But I know. I'm off away from people four—six months at a stretch. Always on the move. Wouldn't make any difference to me if I had a Key or not. Love the work, be doing it anyway. And it's just like anything where you don't see someone for a long time. You notice the differences. And I've seen them."

"Seen them?" murmured Kil.

"Seen them—hell, yes. I've seen them. Jittery, wall-stupid, jumping from city to city as if their tails were on fire—hey boy, you're going to sleep, sit up—and not knowing Sunday from shaving lotion about anything you can't get by pressing a button. Last time I was down below Chilpancingo I saw an orchid, a *cattleya*—one of the common ones, but I took a fancy to it and sealed it in some transparent plastic. Happened a month or so later I was in Mexico—Mexico City, that is—I brought Hortense into a parts place to get the floater rollers degummed. Man in charge happened to see the *cattelya*. Regular native type, too. 'Migawd,' he said—or something to that effect—'What've you got here? Something valuable? Because if it is, you better let me lock it up while the rollers are being cleaned.' Something valuable! Lock it up! His great-grandmother would have known what it was, all right."

"Yes," said Kil.

"Everybody walking around like they were in lockstep. Sure, Files, they say, and the Police. Don't you think it, boy. You know with four billion people in the world, we've got more open country than we had fifty years ago? People've hypnoed themselves into believing the world's all city. Free Transportation. They can go anywhere on Earth they want. And where do they go? From hotel Bungo in Bongo-Bongo to hotel Zenobia in Zanesville. And they say—'how nice,' they say, *'This little suite has just the same number of windows that we had in the one in Bongo-Bongo. My, what a nice permanent feeling it does give one.'* " The old man's voice, which had soared into a savagely mincing falsetto, dropped back to his ordinary tones again. "Hell, people used to save all their lives just so they could get out and see what the rest of the world looked like. And these—" words failed him.

"No good—no use—" muttered Kil, wearily. "Give up."

"Did I say that?" the old man caught him up sharply. "No such thing! While there's life, there's hope; and don't you forget that. Just that people don't budge until they have to, that's all. Most of them just put off doing something about a bad situation until the last moment. What it needs is someone to come along and yank them out of their plastic and concrete. Take them out and rub their noses in the dirt and open their eyes to the good green earth again. Hell, boy, we still got sunsets and thundershowers. And the Grand Canyon, the Amazon, the Sahara, Mount Everest and the Bering Straits. They haven't torn down the Acropolis or the Pyramids. Just nobody goes to look at them for the same reason that people never stepped across town to look at Grant's Tomb. They could go there anytime they wanted to, so they never got around to it. If I had my way—here's Duluth coming up now, boy. Where do you want me to drop you off?"

Kil roused himself with an effort.

"Oh—the terminal," he said, thickly. "I'll have to reset my Key."

"Whatever you want. Going on up the lake, myself," said the old man. He rolled the bug across the wide expanse of the outcity traffic circle and parking area; and let Kil off at curbside before the doors of the terminal. "Good luck, boy."

"Why—thanks," said Kil. "The same to you."

The botanician laughed.

"I got it already. So long."

He geared the bug and rolled off. Kil turned and entered the door behind him.

A mag ship had just unloaded at the terminal and there were lines in front of all the check stations. Kil stood and waited his turn until he could thrust his Key into a check box. Finally it came, there was an almost soundless click and the figures 182 days, 9 hours, popped into sight on the dial of the Key, that being his authorized six month period minus the five days and fifteen hours he had already spent in Duluth during the previous six months. He was turning away from the check box when he felt a touch on his shoulder. He turned to confront a World Policeman in working uniform.

"Kil Bruner?" asked the Policeman.

"That's right," answered Kil.

"I've got an order for an emergency request stability check on you. Will you come to Headquarters, please?"

Kil stared. The man's words rang in his ears without meaning.

"Request emergency check?" he echoed. "Me?"

"Yes, Mr. Bruner."

"But I—" Kil scowled. "I haven't done anything to require an emergency check."

"Sorry, sir, all I know about is the order."

Bewildered, Kil followed the Policeman out of the Terminal to a Police aircar. On the way, he became conscious suddenly of glances here and there from people they were passing. Possibly these same people would have stared at anybody they saw in the company of a Policeman; but Kil felt all at once that the eyes of the world were upon him and condemning him, sight unseen.

In the car he asked the Policeman.

"Have they been looking for me long?"

"I wouldn't know, sir," said the Policeman, gazing out the window.

The rest of the ride was a silent one.

The aircar passed in through one of the gates and settled down finally before a long, low building. Kil got out and the Policeman escorted him inside. Within, the building was very like the Complaint Section he had been in previously, except that there was a row of closed cubicles facing him instead of open booths. The Policeman led him down the row of cubicles until he came to one with an open door.

"In here," said the Policeman. "You face your Key into the cup in the upper right hand corner of the coder panel."

Kil flushed angrily.

"I know," he snapped. "I've taken my test every year since I was six."

"Yes sir," answered the Policeman, indifferently. Kil went into the cubicle, shutting the door behind him.

He sat down before the bank of keys and held his Key to the cup. Above the coder, on the wall before him, the screen lit up as Files awoke to his presence in the testing room.

"Kil Bruner," the words formed on the screen. "You have been requested to come here for an emergency stability check. The test you are about to take will be evaluated by the circuits designed for that purpose. As soon as the test is concluded, a recommendation will be made both on this screen and on the monitor screen outside if any adjustment in your Class Designation should be made. It will then be up to the Police to act or not on the recommendation as they see fit."

Kil paid little attention. He had read these words yearly for nineteen years. Almost, he could have repeated them from memory, these and the words that followed them.

Before you on the coder are Keys for yes and no

answers, multiple choice answers up to a limit of six choices; and an alphabet keyboard for direct coding. If you wish to answer a question in your own words, use the alphabet keyboard.

There was a slight pause. The screen cleared and then lit up again.

Check begun:

The two words were replaced by the first question.

You are a mnemonics engineer?

Kil selected a button and pressed it.

"Yes."

Do you like your work?

"Yes."

Have you ever preferred any other kind of work?

"No."

The questions and answers continued. Kil answered automatically, for these were the standard questions asked in every check. Files was authenticating the data on him that it already had on record. Soon enough, the questions began to break into new territory and narrow down on his present situation.

The Police have taken note recently that you have been occupying yourself in an unusual manner. Have you any explanation for this? Please answer at length, using alphabet keyboard.

Kil moved his fingers down from the yes and no buttons, and typed.

"I've been trying to find my wife."

How did you become separated from your wife?

Kil felt weary. He rubbed a hand slowly across his eyes, and typed.

"Files already has that information."

That is correct. Do you wish to add to or alter your previous account of your wife's disappearance?

"No."

You are concerned about your wife's disappearance?

"Yes."

Do you consider, flashed the screen, *that your search for her is more important than the time and funds you are expending in pursuit of it?*

"Yes." Kil jabbed savagely at the button.

Have you considered the ill effect on your work, of this search? With a sudden sense of shock, Kil remembered the manufactory of coding equipment at Geneva, where he should have arrived ready for work the day following Ellen's disappearance. He had never stopped to think of it; and now, with the time elasped, they would have found another engineer for their current problem. He set his jaw somewhat grimly.

"Yes," he punched. "Yes."

If you were to be informed by authorities that your wife could not be found, would you persist in searching yourself?

"Yes."

If you were informed by the World Police that your continuing search was at variance with the general welfare, would you persist?

"Yes."

Do you consider finding your wife to be more important than a possible defiance of the authority of World Police?

"Yes."

Do you consider finding your wife to be of more

importance than the preservation of general peace?"

Kil hesitated. The screen flashed again.

Would you persist in searching for your wife if Files were to inform you now that by doing so you were endangering the continuing peace of the world?

Kil stiffened in his chair. This was the question. His hand went out to hover over the no button, then stopped. There was no point in putting it off. Files would keep after him with cross questions. Besides, he was not unashamed of the truth. His finger punched down.

"Yes."

The screen cleared and flashed on another line.

Check concluded.

The lights in the cubicle went on. The two words on the screen were replaced by three lines.

Findings of the emergency request Stability check show Kil Bruner, Key 3, 526, 849, 110 to show indications of instability and liable to criminal defiance of authority. Recommend reclassification to Unstab. Class Two.

The screen cleared itself and faded to an unlit grey. Kil rose to his feet and stumbled out.

"Give me your Key," said the Policeman, who had been waiting outside the cubicle.

Kil was too numb to notice that the other no longer said "sir."

CHAPTER TWELVE

Kil stood in the terminal to which the Police aircar had returned him. His Key felt strange on his wrist; and he looked at it. Twenty-one days, read the calchronometer. The sight of the numbers brought on something like a feeling of panic. To a man who had been all the days of his life with his Key fastened to him, to be reclassified downward was like dying in a small fashion. A partial death-sentence. He had a feeling, none the less powerful for being illusory, that part of his time to live had been taken from him. He stood, irresolute.

About him, the hurrying crowds of the terminal swarmed and passed. And, gradually as he stood there, the sense of his difference—now—began to take hold of him. Now and then, one of those passing glanced at him curiously; and he shrank, internally, from that same glance, as he had shrunk earlier when the Policeman had escorted him across the floor to the aircar. As before when he had imagined that their looks assumed the fact that he was a hunted criminal, now he felt irrationally convinced that each one looking at him knew that he had been reclassified, knew that he was now Unstab.

And—because he was himself—a harsh and bristling anger rose within him, against them, against the hurrying multitude, against all Stabs. It came home to him then with a shock that this was what it must be that drove the Unstabs away from the Stabs, into the Slum areas, where they would be at least among their own kind. In the Slums, there would be no need to imagine contempt. You were among equals. And, hating himself for doing it, but realizing the necessity with the thought, Kil turned slowly and headed for the moving roadway that would carry him back to the area from which, with Dekko's help, he had escaped only a few days earlier.

From the Terminal, it was not far. In fact, the Terminal all but touched the Slums. Kil rode in and registered in the first hotel he came to. It struck him as he did so, that he was getting low on money again. He tried to remember, offhand, how much remained in his registered account, but the memory would not come to him without effort and he did not want to make the effort. He put the matter aside.

He was deadly tired. His body seemed a heavy, useless burden for his weary will to drag forward. He went directly up to his room after registering and fell asleep, though it was still only mid-afternoon.

He awoke with a start about sunset. The last, thin, red rays of twilight were coming in through the unopaqued window of his bedroom, making it a place of strange rusty, dying light and tricky shadows. For a moment, he could not think what had brought him so suddenly out of sleep, and then became conscious of someone in the room with him.

He turned his head. Someone was sitting in a chair pulled close beside his bed. In the gloom, Kil made out the facial features with difficulty.

It was the old man. The same one who had taken Ellen away from him.

"Hello Kil," said the old man.

Kil stared at him. The thought came to him that he should leap out of bed and grab this intruder and hang on to him tightly, hold him as ransom for Ellen's return. But his body seemed asleep and separate from his mind. Even his emotions seemed lulled and slumbering.

"Kil," said the old man, "you can't go on like this."

Kil moved his lips with effort. The words came out like a sigh.

"Why not?"

"You're trying the impossible," said the old man, gently. "You can't ever find us. You only hurt yourself by searching. Look at you, worn out in body and mind, broke from your Class A status to an Unstab classification. Give up, Kil."

"Not," whispered Kil, "until I find Ellen."

"You can't, Kil. Ellen's gone where you can never find her. It's like hungering after someone who's dead."

"No!" whispered Kil, stubbornly.

"Yes, Kil. You don't understand. Somehow, a

mistake happened. Something went wrong. Somehow you saw Ellen walk off with me. That's the only reason I'm here now. To you, like everyone else there, it should have seemed that she just vanished, suddenly, without a trace.''

"What—happened?''

"We stopped time there for a moment, Kil. Or rather, we speeded it up a great deal for ourselves, alone. You shouldn't have been able to see us go; but you did.''

"She—'' Kil struggled with a great effort of pushing the words past his lips. "She didn't want to go.''

"But Ellen knew she had to. Kil—'' the old man put his hand on Kil's shoulder. "Ellen always knew the time had to come when she'd have to leave you. She never really belonged to you completely. Think of her as of something you loved very much that was merely lent to you for a while and then taken back again.''

"No,'' whispered Kil. "We didn't marry that way. It wasn't something temporary.''

"It was for Ellen.''

"I don't believe you,'' whispered Kil.

"It was.''

"No,'' Kil struggled to make the thin thread of sound come stronger from his lips, but could not. "And anyway, it wasn't for me. It's too late now to tell me it was supposed to have been temporary. I should've been told at the start.''

"Ellen couldn't tell you. The secret wasn't hers to tell.''

"What secret? The Project? Sub-E?''

The old man leaned forward in the dimness.

"What's that?" he said, sharply. "Where did you hear that?"

"Is it?"

"Answer me, Kil!"

"No, you answer me. First. Why should it always be your way? What do I owe you? You took Ellen."

"I didn't take her, Kil. She went of her own free will."

"She didn't want to go." A deep fury stirred slowly and distantly in Kil, held down by the same thing that was sapping his strength.

"She was unhappy at saying goodbye to you," said the old man, "but she wanted to go. She knew she had to go. She has work to do."

"It's not true."

"Yes," insisted the old man. "It is true. You must believe that, Kil, and stop this hopeless search of yours. You're hurting yourself—and you're hurting Ellen."

"She—knows?"

"Yes," said the old man, grudgingly.

A great and powerful feeling of joy that was somehow separate from that part of him that was being held in thrall, flamed up in Kil.

"Let her come and tell me herself, then," he whispered. "Let her come and tell me to stop trying to find her."

"She can't come."

"You mean you won't let her come."

"She mustn't. She knows she mustn't."

"Because she doesn't dare. Let her come to me and she'd stay with me. Wouldn't she?"

"No," said the old man. "No! For your own

sake, Kil, you mustn't believe that. She's gone
from you and from this world of yours. I tell you,
as surely as if she were dead."

"She's not dead. She's living and I'll find her.
Do you hear? I'll find her if I have to take the world
apart stick by stick and stone by stone. I'll find her
if I have to blow the universe apart and hunt for
her among the pieces. Do you hear me? *Do you
hear me? DO YOU HEAR ME?*"

And suddenly, all restraint vanished, Kil was
sitting up in the bed and shouting with the full
power of his voice. His cries clashed and echoed
in the empty room.

And the old man was gone.

Quickly, Kil began to dress. When he was
through, he walked to the door of the suite and
turned the apartment's sunbeams down and out
even as they were waxing against the falling
night. He paused a moment, looking into the
shadows.

"I love you, Ellen," he said softly.

Then he went out.

It was full evening by the time he stepped out
on the street. The lights of the area were on,
throwing the sky into a deeper blackness above
him. He took the moving roadway toward the part
of the area where he had first gone, back in the
beginning when he had come looking for the Ace
King. And, as he went, he opened a door in his
mind that had been some time closed, and set the
dusty machinery that he found there, once more
to work.

Kil was a mnemonics engineer. His particular
field was the formulating of memory systems for

specialized jobs; but before he had qualified for this, he had gone through all the necessary elementary and advanced courses in memory training that were prerequisites to the six years' study of discriminative techniques in mnemonics. The associative functions and the formulae of procedure were as much a part of him as the muscle training that enabled him to walk surefootedly upon the earth. Now he turned these mental tools to the task of ferreting out the secrets of whatever had taken Ellen from him. Mali had said that, buried somewhere in the memories of the last five years, when Kil had been married to Ellen, were clues that would lead him to her. Mali could not find these clues, even under hypnotic search. But he, Kil, could find them. If they were there, he could find them. Because it was his mind; and no one could know it like himself. He could not only remember, but having remembered, he could study the memory, discovering in it things he had not noticed the first time, until it was squeezed dry of every elemental drop of information within it.

There had been a breeze from the mainland, from the hills of Kowloon, that day in Hong Kong, when he had first seen Ellen. She had been standing on the balcony of the Hotel Royal and she . . .

. . . The sights and sounds and smells of memory rose like incense in the back of Kil's mind. Silently, he tiptoed his conscious attention out of the room of his past, leaving it to work its wonders in its own way; and closed the door upon it.

He looked up. The more recent memory of the bar front he had seen on his first trip to this Unstab district clicked sharply into identification with the bar front coming at him, down the street. He waited until the roadway brought him opposite, then stepped off on the departure rollers to the side, walked across the short strip of unmoving cement, and pressed his Key into the door cup.

It opened; and he entered.

The bar had not changed. Nor the people inside it. Individual faces were different, but the collective face was the same. As Kil came in, most of the drinkers glanced up; but this time, only momentarily. Dekko's lessons had been effective upon Kil. The faces returned to their glasses and the pause in the conversation was buried and forgotten in a fresh wave of murmuring voices.

There was a new bartender behind the bar. Kil walked up to him. Neatly, out of one compartment in his ordered memory vault, Kil selected slang terms necessary to the occasion.

"Yeah, Chief?" said the bartender as he came up. "What?"

He was a man of average height with slightly lumpy features. Almost insolently at ease, he leaned on the bar.

"Dosker me someone," said Kil. He reached in his pocket for a roll of dollars, tore off five of them and slid them across the bar. "The name is Dekko."

The bartender rolled the strip of soft metal tabs up into a tight cylinder and stuck it in his tunic pocket.

"Just Dekko?" he said. "No nut to that bolt?"

"Dekko," said Kil.

The bartender moved a little down the bar and

fiddled with something underneath. "Not one,"
he said, after a moment. "Any other towns you
want to dosker? Give you five for twenty."

"No," Kil shook his head. "He'll be showing.
How much for a local look?"

"How long a look?"

"For the next week—seven days."

"Fifty for the spotter, twenty-five for the contact, and twenty-five for me. And the Ace'll take
twenty per cent. One-deuce-and-big-O."

Kil took out a roll of twenties and tore off a
hundred and twenty dollars worth. The bartender
gathered them in.

"Who's Ace now?" Kil asked.

"Garby. Been on three days."

Kil felt a small relief. He had been bracing himself against contact with the Ace he had run from
before, even though Dekko had told him that such
men very seldom stayed in one area even the full
length of time allowed them by their classification. He turned as the bartender leaned down
behind the bar and in a low voice put out the call
for Dekko that Kil had just paid for. Kil felt satisfaction. Inside of a few minutes all the public
places in the Unstab area would be notified that
there was a reward for spotting the little man and
notifying Kil of his whereabouts.

He turned back to the bar again.

"Coffee," he said to the bartender. The lumpy
features showed amazement.

"You mean a stim?"

"Just coffee," repeated Kil. The bartender
stared for a second, but then turned and dialed his
selector. After a second, there was delivery be-

neath the bar and he lifted a cup and thermopot up in front of Kil.

Kil paid and, taking the two items, walked back to a table in one of the dark little recesses along the further wall. He sat down.

He poured his coffee black, ignoring the cream and sugar bulges on the container's side. Sipping at the dark, hot liquid, he set himself to think.

CHAPTER THIRTEEN

"WELL, do us, riggers! Looks like we hit the doby prize!"

Kil came back to himself with a start and looked up. Three men had just come in the door of the bar and were staring at him. Two of them were Unstabs he had never seen before, but the third was the tall, blond, drunken boy who had yelled "Big S!" at Kil the time before in the bar.

Only now the boy was sober.

He came toward Kil, the two behind him, following. He reached Kil's table and leaned on it with both hands.

"Hello S." he said. His eyes, blue and bright and small in comparison with the rest of his otherwise goodlooking face, carefully scanned Kil, clothes and expression. "Or are you still S., Juby?"

Silently, Kil tilted the Key on his wrist so that the other could read the classification on its face.

"Two!" said the boy. "Well, Two! Big S. into

Two goes once. I suppose you think that makes you one of us riggers, don't you?"

Kil still said nothing. His mind was working swiftly and calmly, but a hot coal was fanning itself into burning anger inside him.

"Well, it don't!" said the boy, thrusting out his jaw and pushing his face so close to Kil that Kil could see the white, curling hair in his nostrils. "You're still S. to me, Juby. And you know what we do to S's down here. We shake them out."

"Juby," said the boy. "Juby, I'm talking to you. And I want an answer."

Kil threw the coffee in the boy's face; and followed that with the cup itself at one of the two others. He flipped the table in front of him, over against them and jumped to his feet. Then, taking advantage of the confusion, he thew himself at them.

He punched low, and his fist sank into the blond boy's stomach. Kicking out blindly, he connected with the ankle of one of the others; and that one went down, abruptly, hitting his head on the floor with an ugly, thick, cracking sound. I've killed him, thought Kil seeing the man sprawl limply and lie still. But then he had no more time to think, because the third man was on top of him.

The third man was small and hard. He literally tried to climb up Kil's tall body, chopping viciously with the side of his right hand as he did so. Kil, all fear lost now in the pure white flame of battle, wrenched him free and swung wildly at his face. The fist missed, but his elbow did not, and the man went down, blood spurting from nose and mouth.

Staggering, with a tingling elbow, Kil felt a sudden heavy blow low on the back of his head, which drove him forward, tottering, until a nearby table blocked his progress and kept him from falling forward on his face. He rolled to the right, just as the heavy body of the blond boy drove past him and crashed into the table where Kil had been. Kil swung with all his strength at the averted jaw of the boy, but the blow missed and skidded off the other's shoulder as he turned to face Kil.

Kil threw himself forward, head low. He butted the blond boy high on the chest and they both crashed to the floor, rolling over and over among the chair and table legs, both struggling to get their arms free to fight and at the same time keep their opponent's arms imprisoned. Kil could feel the blond boy's legs trying for a scissors grip around his waist. A fragment from a near-forgotten history of flatboating on the Mississippi nearly three hundred years before came to him. *Bite his ear*, he thought. And with grim relish, he did. The blond boy screamed like a hurt animal and by mutual consent they rolled apart and staggered to their feet.

The blond boy was frantically pawing through his clothing. Abruptly, he stopped and ran across to the man who had knocked himself out on the floor. Flinging his hand into the recumbent one's tunic, he pulled out a thin cylinder about fifteen centimeters long, which suddenly, in his hand, sprouted a narrow, wavy-edged blade three times its own length. With this weapon, longer than his own forearm, he advanced on Kil.

There was a soft ringing from behind the bar. So incongruous was it in that tense atmosphere that for a moment, everything halted. Kil even turned his head to look; and the blond boy's face swung momentarily and inquiringly in the same direction.

The bartender was nodding his head and listening to something inaudible from below the bar. He looked up suddenly at the blond boy.

"Clab it!" he said. "He's dyked."

The blond boy breathed heavily through his nostrils and swung back to Kil.

"Clab you!" he threw over his shoulder at the bartender. Beside him, the man with the smashed nose was helping the man who had knocked himself unconscious to his feet. The blond boy glanced at them.

"Cover me," he said.

"I tell you he's dyked!" shouted the bartender.

The blond boy fumbled in his tunic and this time found a twin to the cylinder which had sprouted a knife blade in his hand. He tossed it back in the direction of his two friends. "Hold 'em. I'm going to viv this Juby even he's been dyked by Ace himself."

The man with the smashed nose produced his own cylinder and extended its blade. The other man, looking rather sick, picked up the one from the floor and extended it. They moved in to stand with their backs to the blond boy, facing outward to the crowd with their blades ready. The blond boy looked at Kil and grinned in a white, unnatural way, moving the tip of his blade in small, slow circles.

"Ever been vived, Juby?" he said. "Well, now's your time to learn."

"Do me!" cried the bartender in exasperation. He swung furiously about to look up and down the bar. "Singles! Where's a Singles? Pull that dyke for me. It's worth a hundred."

A slim little middle-aged man at the end of the bar slid off his seat, patting his lips dry with a napkin.

"I'm a Singles," he said. From under his chair he drew a slim, limber-looking, highly polished cane about five-sixths of a meter in length. It looked rather like the sort of swagger stick affected by ornate dressers, with evening clothes. With mincing steps, he approached the three men holding knives and stopped a little more than his own length from them.

"All right viv-boys," he said. "Fun's done."

The two friends of the blond boy stirred uneasily.

"Hey, Fabe," the man with the smashed nose said to him, "let's slip. It's not worth the fun."

The blond boy, however, had turned slowly to face the middle-aged man; and his face still held that unnaturally white look.

"What's loose in your guts?" he said to his friend. "There's three of us."

"But there's no room, Fabe," said the third man.

"Do me!" murmured the blond. "Who needs room?" he snarled suddenly at the other two. "Who do you want to take—him with me, or me by yourselves?"

Reluctantly, the other two turned toward the little man. As if this had been a signal, the stick in the little man's hand suddenly blurred into a spinning fan of motion as he twirled it in a humming circle whose center was his wrist. Like a gauzy blur of motion, it floated beside him, in front of him, flatly over his head. Quite calmly, he walked forward and the three men with knives jumped to meet him.

What followed was too fast for Kil to see in detail. There was a series of sharp, cracking sounds and one of the knife men broke and ran for the door, while the other screamed hoarsely and staggered across the room with his hands pressed to his face and blood seeping from between the fingers.

"I'm blind!" he screamed. "I'm *blind!*"

He collapsed sobbing in a corner. No one paid any attention to him. The blond boy lay still on the floor, face down. Hardly able to believe it was all over, Kil walked slowly forward.

"Thanks," he said to the middle-aged man, who shrugged.

"A job," he answered. He was wiping the metal ferule at the end of his stick, with a handkerchief. "You got the hundred, or do I get it from Drinks?"

Kil reached in his pocket for the money; and, after he had handed it over, turned his attention to the blond boy.

"I'd better get that knife of his while he's out," he said, stooping over.

The Singles stopped him with the end of his cane.

"What for?" he asked. With his foot, he rolled the blond boy over indifferently. The blue eyes were still wide open. They would never close themselves now. The whole right temple above them was caved in as if by a small, blunt hatchet.

Kil stared at the slim, almost toy-like stick in the man's hand with horrified amazement. The man smiled agreeably.

"It's not the single-stick," he said. "It's what you do with it. Any Juby can use a knife." He turned and walked back to the bar. Kil followed him. The bartender leaned across and spoke to Kil.

"Why didn't you call help earlier?" he said. "If I'd known you were willing to pay, I could've tagged Singles for you right away. From the way you talked, I figured you could take care of yourself."

Kil shrugged. Reaction was setting in and he felt too shaky to venture an argument.

"You got dyked by Uncle George," went on the bartender. "Somebody wants to see you."

Kil blinked.

"Uncle George? Who wants to see me?"

"How'd I know who wants to see you?" said the bartender. "Uncle George's a dyker—a bond dyker. Somebody got in touch with him and got you dyked for five thousand worth of trouble money. That's enough to buy you out of anything but a small scale war in this district. You go to your hotel. Uncle George'll meet you there."

Still somewhat dazed, Kil turned away and went slowly to the door and out into the street. He took the roadway toward his hotel.

He reached the hotel without incident. The glass front door opened to his Key and the lobby was deserted. He crossed to the desk. The human clerk was off duty and the simulacrum behind the counter informed him that there had been no messages, or anyone to see him. It stood, a very fine, dapper imitation of a man; but Kil could see, without leaning too far over the counter, the cable that protruded from the desk and attached to its ankle, the cable connecting it with the brain of the hotel. For some reason, although he had seen this sort of thing thousands of times before in his lifetime, it was subtly disturbing tonight to realize the falsity and inhumanity of the imitation before him. And there came back to him, suddenly, something he had heard casually a long time ago: that Unstabs were said to have an unreasoning dislike of automation and anything connected with it. And he wondered for a second if this were symptomatic of some new decay in himself. Then he put the notion from his mind.

The disk elevator was at its ceaseless motion at one end of the lobby. He stepped aboard one of the disks and let it carry him up. At his floor he got off and went down the empty hallway to his room. The door was closed and he faced his Key into the cup. It swung open and he entered.

And stopped.

Across from him, seated in one of the room's armchairs, was a strangely familiar figure. He had seen it once before slumped over a table in the bar he had just left, on a certain occasion as he was following the tall Unstab named Birb out the door to meet Ace. It was the figure of a paunchy man on the brink of old age. He was swathed in heavy tunic, slacks and cape, and his face had a red, doughy consistency as he smiled at Kil.

"You're Uncle George?" asked Kil, all but sure
of his visitor, but brought to caution by the experience he had just passed.

Uncle George opened his mouth and laughed.
"Sometimes," he answered, "but not always."
And the voice was the voice of Dekko.

CHAPTER FOURTEEN

KIL stared at him. The disguise was so good he found himself doubting his ears.

"Dekko?" he said, at last, wonderingly.

"Me," said the voice of Dekko, as sharp and wise as ever and coming with incongruous effect from the soft aging-man's face. The wrinkled hands went up under the double chin, fumbled and pulled. The whole face seemed to crumple and pull upward; and Dekko skinned off an amazing flesh-tight mask that varied from tissue thinness in spots to thicknesses of an inch or more in others. "Sit, Kil, while I seal this place."

He got up and moved quickly across the room to the door. He produced what seemed to be a small duplicate of the clock-like mechanism Kil had seen on the inner surface of the door to Mali's study, and pressed it against the crack between door and jamb, where it stuck.

"That'll scramble anything," he said with satisfaction. "And there's no loopers. I checked. Find yourself a chair, like I said, Kil. We got some talking to do."

Kil dropped into a chair. Dekko came back and sat down opposite him.

"How'd you get away?" Kil asked.

"This," Dekko poked his finger at the mask. "It never pays to run, Kil. It's always better to stand still and look like something else. I made it over the fence and changed in a ditch. Then walked, not ran to the nearest Terminal. So now it's Uncle George until the pressure goes down."

A note of wryness in the last words make Kil look more closely at him.

"I got you into something more than you bargained for, didn't I?"

"Yes and no," Dekko smiled. "I'd always wanted to take a crack at the O.T.L.—oh, found out what it means, by the way. Organizational Tacticians' League. That's a mouthful to mean nothing, isn't it? Yeah, I always wanted to try them. Nobody's fault they turned out tougher than I thought."

"But now," Kil looked at him steadily, "you've come around to tell me you can't have anything more to do with me."

"No," Dekko shook his head. "Can't abandon a client. Ruin my business reputation. Just got to figure a way to get Mali off our necks besides finding your wife, that's all."

"Mali told me he thought you might be one of McElroy's men," said Kil, bluntly.

Dekko grinned merrily.

"Maybe I am, Kil, maybe I am." His voice and

face were perfectly opaque to any clues hidden behind them. "Now don't try to fish me. It won't do you any good to start with. And to finish, I got my own reasons for what I do. All you got to know is that I'm on your side."

"What can you do for me now?" said Kil.

"I can keep you alive," retorted the little man. "How close were you to being viv meat less than an hour ago?"

Kil nodded.

"That's right—thanks."

"Nothing. Now let's forget it and get down to business." He hunched forward in the chair. "From what I can scrape up, your wife is hooked into something big. Right?"

"Yes," said Kil.

"It's something called The Project; and something else called Sub-E. Check?"

Kil nodded. Dekko looked thoughtful.

"I'll tell you one thing, Kil," he said. "I didn't hear about those two myself until just back a ways—me, who has to know everything for my job's sake. Now just what would you suppose they'd be?"

Kil shook his head.

"I don't know." He considered for a moment the possible effect of the information on Dekko, before adding. "Mali wants to make sure it isn't something that can stop him. He's planning to try and take control of Files and the world away from the Police."

"Oh? What all did he say?" asked Dekko, and Kil told him everything that had been done and said from the moment of his capture until his

escape. When he had finished, Dekko twisted his
lips humorlessly.

"That twist," he commented. "He's as bad as
his sister. They're both scrambled eggs."

A memory of something he had seen flashed out
of the storehouse of Kil's trained mind.

"You're wrong about that part of it," he said. "I
got a look at his Key. It's Class A."

"Down one for you," replied Dekko, promptly.
"Don't you know about that part of it? Mali
couldn't run that O.T.L. of his without some way
to beat the residence check. In that outfit, they
trade Keys."

Kil stared.

"Trade Keys? They can't do that."

"Why not?" said Dekko, "if they got someone
willing to trade with them? There's all kinds of
kick societies. Some of them trade more'n Keys.
But to get back to it here—there's this Project and
the O.T.L. wants it. They think they got a wire to
it through you to your wife?"

"Yes," Kil drew a deep breath. "And I think
perhaps they're right.

"She's in it, you mean?"

"Ellen? Yes—I think so." On sudden impulse,
Kil found himself telling Dekko about the latest
visit from the old man. When he was finished the
little man nodded gravely.

"It all ties in then," he said. He nodded as if to
himself and then looked sharply at Kil. "That
brings us to what I've got to tell you. You've got an
invitation."

"Invitation?"

"To a talk with Mali. No wires. Everything out
in the open."

Kil looked at him in astonishment.

"How—" he said; and fumbled. "I thought you were hiding out from Mali."

Dekko laughed silently.

"Do me, Kil!" he said. "Mali didn't have to meet me face to face to let me know this. He just spread the word around where he knew I'd find it."

"What word?" Kil was bewildered.

"The word that he wanted to talk with you. He's made up his mind he can't make you help him unless you want to. So he'd like to try offering you enough to make it worthwhile for you to help him."

"No!" said Kil, violently. "I'll see him—"

"Hold on, Kil," Dekko checked him. "Anything wrong with getting him off your neck if it's possible? And he may offer you something you'd want."

"He can't offer me Ellen. That's all I want."

"No, but maybe he could offer to help you get her back. That'd be worth something, wouldn't it?"

"Maybe," said Kil, yielding only slightly.

"All right. Let's sit back again and add up what we've got. Now, as I see it—" Dekko's dark eyes narrowed thoughtfully, shrewdly, his thin, hungry face contrasting almost ludicrously with the fake paunchiness of his disguised body below it, like a knife blade protruding from a suety lump of fat. "We've got a three way pull for power here. We got the Police trying to hold the lid on, same as always. We got the O.T.L. trying to push the lid off and climb up on top where the Sticks are now. And we got this Project bunch with plans nobody knows, but something powerful everybody

wants, sort of sitting pat in the background. How's
that sound to you?"

"Yes. That's it," said Kil. "At least, that's the
way it looks to me, too."

"Now, your wife's mixed up with this third
bunch, this Project. That's clear. And Mali thinks
maybe you can find her and by sticking with you,
he can locate the Project when you do. All right.
Now, two questions. How does Mali think you can
find her when you haven't been able to so far?"
Dekko stared sharply at Kil.

"I told you that. He thinks that in the five years
we were married I picked up information from
Ellen without realizing it, to lead us to the Project,
or tell us what it is."

"What do you think?"

"Maybe," said Kil, grimly. "Anyway I'm trying." He made an attempt to explain something of
the mnemonic techniques involved, but they
were clearly outside Dekko's sphere of knowl-
edge.

"Let that part slide," said the little man, at last.
"I'll take your word for it. Maybe you can do it.
Now, the question is, if that's the situation, is it a
good idea to see Mali after all?"

"I might learn something from him," said Kil.
He rubbed his chin. "The hell of it is, right now I
don't know. I haven't any idea of what I ought to
be looking for in these memories."

"Nobody else knows either, looks like," said
Dekko.

"That's true."

"Well," Dekko got to his feet and slipped the
face mask back into position. At once, he seemed

again a stranger, and it was hard to believe the familiar voice coming from such a patent unknown. "You catch some rest. It'll take a little while to wire a contact with Mali. I'll see if I can't get him back here by noon tomorrow. All right?"

Kil nodded and stood up.

"Don't take any chances you don't have to," he said.

"Do me!" the pudgy features grinned at him. "You think I lived the last thirty years on luck?"

Dekko—or Uncle George, rather—went toward the door. Kil followed and opened it for him.

"Wait—" said Kil, suddenly, as the little man was about to leave. "You said two questions. What's the other?"

"Oh, that—" Dekko looked up at him. "Just, that if this Sub-E the Project's got is so much a thing as everybody thinks it is, how come the Project hasn't been using it for its own wants before this? Or is it?"

It was, Kil realized, a good question. A very good question indeed.

CHAPTER FIFTEEN

KIL awoke feeling rested, but puzzled. Dekko's last question of the night before was still swimming annoyingly around in his head. It was something that had not occurred to him at all before; but now it clung to the focal spot of his attention. Why indeed, if this mysterious Project had the power everyone seemed to be giving it credit for having, hadn't it taken an active hand in the goings on, before this? Why had the old man only reasoned with him, Kil, instead of taking definite action to stop him? Was it because of Ellen?

The more Kil pondered it, the more the unreasoning conviction began to grow on him that the situation as he saw it was only bits and pieces of something much bigger out of sight. Something of which the Police, the O.T.L., the Project, himself, Ellen, Dekko, and all the rest were only parts. He had the feeling of being advanced and withdrawn according to some obscure master plan—not the plan of another character, as Mali had said, but that of some strange sort of Fate. He searched through a strange shadow land of mighty and hidden purposes. Even now, sitting here in this hotel suite, there seemed to come to him a weird sense of contact, of interlocking purpose with people elsewhere, everywhere, in the city, in the world, in the . . .

In the . . . ? His mind groped into nothingness.

He was still reaching out for he knew not what, when Dekko arrived. The little man looked at him with sharp curiosity.

"Morning," he said. "What's on your mind?"

"I don't know," Kil said slowly. He sat up in the chair and noticed abruptly that Dekko was once more undisguised. "What happened to Uncle George?"

"I'm part of your deal with Mali for a talk. Simple enough. Anything new crop up since last night?"

Kil shook his head. "Mali's coming here to see me, is he?"

"Any minute—" the doorbell chimed. "Right on the dot. I knew he was just behind me." Dekko got up and went across the room to open the door. Mali came in, followed by Melee. It was a shock to Kil to see her with him. She did not speak to Kil, but looked at him with silent eyes out of a face that was all the more beautiful for its unusual paleness.

"Hello, Kil," said Mali, cheerfully. He ignored Dekko. "Nice of you to agree to see us."

"Sit down," said Kil.

They took seats. Mali, directly before Kil; Melee, a little back as if she would hold herself outside the sphere of their conversation. Mali smiled.

"You surprised us all by running off," he said.
"How on earth did you manage it? Breaking conditioning like that is supposed to be just about
impossible."

His voice was warm and eager, his face almost
admiring. It was as if he was congratulating Kil on
some extraordinary and laudable accomplishment, in the spirit of true sportsmanship.

"I found out I could get away," said Kil, "so I
did."

Mali shook his head.

"It certainly shook things up. I wish I'd known
you could do that beforehand."

"You aren't going to tell me," said Kil, looking
straight at him, "that you'd have acted differently?"

"I might have. I had to try you out, you know. I
can apologize if you want. Not that it means much
in this affair."

"No." Kil shifted a little impatiently in his
chair. "Well, what's this you wanted to talk to me
about?"

"Dekko didn't tell you?"

"Suppose you tell me."

"Of course. Oh, by the way. I just thought I'd ask
you about the conditioning. The loyalty to me, for
example. How it could be there one minute and
then all gone the next. It is—all gone, I suppose?"
And Mali's eyes fixed suddenly and unshakably
on Kil's.

As a matter of fact, it was not. Kil suddenly
recognized the quicksand into which Mali's casu-
alness had been leading him. At the direct question a remnant of the conditioned emotion

threatened to rise within him, but he thrust it violently back.

"All gone," he said.

"And—your affection for Melee? All gone?"

In spite of himself, Kil looked at the girl. She gazed back at him with a look neither of appeal nor command, but of something like sadness. An odd pity stirred inside him and he felt the edge of the quicksand crumbling away under his feet.

"I don't love her," he said coldly; and Melee's eyes dropped.

"Yes. Well—" there was now a slight dryness to Mali's tone. "Well, I just thought I'd try that avenue, though I didn't have any real hopes of it leading to anything. Now, to business. I'm willing to cooperate, Kil, if you are."

"What kind of cooperate?"

"I mean what I say. I want that Project and I think you're the man to help me get it. Not that I'm convinced it's any real danger to me, but I believe in playing safe. Help me; I'm willing to make it worthwhile for you."

"Go on," said Kil.

Mali put his hands on his knees and leaned forward. The personality of the man came through to Kil like a compelling force.

"The shift in power from the Police to me is inevitable, Project or no Project. As I told you, in the combined Societies, I've got a group of over fifty million adults—that's one out of every eighty humans on the globe. And they each influence up to a half a dozen more outside the Societies. That's an overwhelming minority, the way the world is set up today. So you can take it as a virtual certainty that you and your wife will eventually be living in a world that I control. Now, I can determine whether your life in that world will be pleasant or unpleasant; or whether you'll be allowed to exist in it at all. And I'll guarantee the pleasantness if you'll cooperate."

He stopped. Kil waited a minute.

"Is that it?" he said.

"Except to be specific. What I'm offering you will be equal rights and privileges with any member of the O.T.L., when the time comes. That means the best possible life, once we're in power. And security."

"And *that's* it?"

"That's it." Mali sat back.

"All right," said Kil. He leaned forward in his turn. "You say it's inevitable that your group takes over. I don't think so."

Mali spread his hands, wordlessly.

"In the first place," went on Kil. "You say you've got fifty million people behind you. I'll take your word on that, though just for the sake of argument. What makes you sure you're going to hang on to them? What if you didn't?"

"Kil, what's to stop me?" asked Mali. "It's not just the Societies. People in general are sick of Files and the Police. Everyone knows that. And I don't need five million, let alone fifty, to overthrow the Police. Only it's going to turn out, after I've done it, that those who belong to my Societies are the favored ones under the new setup. Who won't hop on the bandwagon then?"

"And what if someone starts building CH bombs with no Police to stop them?"

Mali laughed.

"Kil—" he said, gently. "You don't think I'm

fool enough to do away with Files and the Police in actuality? No, we just change the names. Put our own personnel in the Police posts. Relax the residence limits a little and say that we can't give up our Keys all at once because Society's geared to them." He laughed again. "You're an amateur at this business, Kil. Don't you know that real revolutions never work? Only the fake ones. Turn the whole world topsy-turvy and everybody gets hurt. But if it's well planned, you can make a minor adjustment up at the top levels without disturbing the machinery at all."

He smiled at Kil.

"Consider my bandwagon," he said.

"I'm considering the Project's," replied Kil.

Mali sobered all at once.

"What do you mean by that?" he asked.

"Just that I think it's pretty sure the Project's got a bandwagon, too," said Kil. "That name of theirs implies action of some kind. And what I've seen of them makes it look like an organization—a pretty successful organization, since you haven't been able to lay your hands on it, with all your fifty millions. Maybe the Project plans to take over the world. Have you thought of that?"

"Yes," said Mali, slowly. "I thought of it. I was hoping you hadn't."

"I have," Kil watched him closely. "And as long as there's that possibility, it strikes me I might be better off with them, especially since my wife seems already well connected with them."

"Yes," Mali's voice was calm. "Maybe you might." He slid a hand into a pocket of his kilt and lay back. "But I don't believe you, Kil. You aren't really considering which is the wisest move for you. You've never actually had any idea of joining me, because actually you're a man of unreasoning prejudices and loyalties, and the fact that your wife belongs to an opposite side outweighs any logic I could show you. So—"

"A looper!" shouted Dekko, suddenly. "Look out! He must have rode in on one of you. Get him!"

He flung out his arm, indicating a small beetle clinging high on the wall in one corner of the room. At the same time he swept up an ashtray in his other hand and threw it. It smashed squarely on the insect and both dropped.

"Come on!" cried Dekko, pulling Kil from the chair. "Run!" He yanked Kil in the direction of the door to the hallway of the hotel, through which Mali and Melee were already scrambling. The four of them tumbled out into the hall.

"There they are!" yelped Dekko, as two heads wearing the riot helmets of a World Police raiding squad appeared around one end of the corridor. Mali's hand came out of his tunic pocket with a small gun which spat silver streaks in their direction. There were several loud explosions at the end of the corridor and chunks were blown out of the walls. The two heads ducked back.

"This way!" hissed Dekko in Kil's ear. Kil hesitated.

"The elevator!"

There was the sound of slow, heavy footsteps in a momentary silence, and slowly around the end of the corridor, two new figures came into view. There were a couple of other Police, in laborious movement with guns in their hands and the glassy sheen of phase shield body armor about them. They almost bumped shoulders as they rounded the corner and blundered hastily apart as the two shields touched for a fraction of a second and arced viciously.

"Not the elevator! They can cut power. Come on!" And, taking advantage of the reeling Policeman's momentary confusion, Dekko pulled Kil down the corridor at a run in the opposite direction and around the safety of another corner, as Mali and Melee leaped for the elevator.

They passed the fire escape tube, an old-fashioned staircase set in a cylinder of asbestoid concrete and running vertically through the center of the building. Kil's hand was on the handle of the heavy door that would give entrance to it, but Dekko still pulled him on.

"Here," he said, a little farther on. He yanked open a small, waist-high door in the wall, revealing two small disk elevators, one rising and one falling, side by side.

"Delivery," said Dekko. "You take the up. Go up two floors and wait. I'll go down a floor and draw them off to the street. Wait five minutes and then go down the fire stair."

Kil nodded. He half-jumped, half-wriggled into the next rising disk. The space was adequate, but cramped, and a slight claustrophobia suffocated him as he rose up the dark shaft. A few seconds later a glimmer of light around the edge of a door warned of the floor above. He let it pass; and went one floor higher before getting off.

On the floor where he emerged, the silence was almost shocking. The carpeted hallway with its softly glowing walls seemed to slumber in a peace unbelievably remote from the recent violence two flights of stairs down. Hurriedly, Kil went along the hall back to the door entering on the fire escape tube. He opened it with caution and stepped through into a different, echoing silence. The slight scrape of his shoe soles on the concrete seemed to shout the news of his presence there. He tiptoed to the stairwell and looked down it, straining his ears.

For a moment, he saw and heard nothing. And then abruptly—he could not tell whether it had been above or below him—there was a sudden blast of shots and cries, cut off as suddenly as they had begun, as if by the momentary opening and closing of a door. Then silence once more.

Kil breathed deeply and leaned against the railing overhanging the stairwell. Some little number of slow seconds went by; and then, slowly, one by one, the sound of footsteps on the stairs above began to descend toward him. The *pat*-pause, *pat*-pause, of someone coming very slowly and hesitantly down.

He glanced down the empty spiral of the staircase and then at his Key. The five minutes Dekko had told him to wait was not yet up. He envisioned one of the men in body armor coming down to him, then changed his mind. The steps were too light. He backed into a corner of the landing and stood waiting, staring up the curve of the stair, where it bent out of sight beyond its own railing and the floor of the curve above him.

Pat-pause, *pat*-pause, *pat*-pause. A head bobbed into sight around the curve of the railing and turned toward him, continuing down. He stood caught in the paralysis of shock. It was Melee.

She did not say anything, or change her pace, but continued to descend toward him at the same slow rate. Her hands were pressed together at a point just below her throat and above her breasts. Her slim, white hands were pale against the soft green of her tunic, and her oval face above them was pale, pale under her auburn hair. She looked at Kil with wide, shocked eyes.

"Melee—" he said, huskily.

She opened her mouth as if to answer him, but she said nothing. She stepped carefully down the last two steps and came slowly to him across the landing. As she reached him, her knees buckled and he caught her, easing her to the landing and himself with her, so that he sat on the top stair, holding her against him. She lay with her head against his chest, still holding her hands pressed tightly to her. Her eyelids fluttered, and she gazed at him with a wondering look.

"Kil—?" she said. It was more a small whimper than a word.

"Melee," he said. "Are you hurt? Let me see."

He pulled her hands away. There was a singed hole in the tunic and a little spot of red. It was high on her chest and did not look serious, but when he tried to open the tunic, she stopped him.

"No," she murmured. "Ugly now. I don't want you to see."

"Melee, we've got to fix it!"

"No," she shook her head slowly, rolling it from side to side. "All gone inside. Don't."

"Wait here," said Kil, trying to stand up. "I'll go get help."

"No. No good." She held to him. "Stay with me, Kil . . . Kil?"

He sat back.

"I'm here."

"Doesn't . . . hurt. . . ."

"Good. That's good, Melee."

She choked; and though she held her lips tightly, a little blood came through. She made a protesting sound. Kil fumbled for a handkerchief and wiped her lips.

"Ugly," she said again. Tears stood suddenly in her eyes. "You never . . . want to kiss me, now."

He bent his head and kissed her lips.

"Oh . . . Kil . . ." the tears spilled over and ran down her cheeks. "Wipe . . ." she said. "Please . . ."

Kil dried her eyes gently with a clean section of the handkerchief.

"Hush," he said. "Don't talk."

"Love you . . . Kil . . ."

"Shh," he said. He kissed her again, and smoothed back the hair from her eyes. A wetness on the hand he pressed against her back, holding her, drew his attention. He lifted it up momentarily, looking at it over her shoulder. There was blood on it. He put it back.

"Hush," he said, again.

"Never liked . . . Mali much . . ." Her face twisted with hurt for a second. "Tried . . ." She was silent for a moment. "My brother . . ." But she did not finish.

Her eyes closed. After a while they flew open suddenly.

"Kil—" she said. "Don't go—"

"I'm not leaving," he said. "I'll stay right here."

She breathed out as if in relief and her eyes closed again. She did not say anything more.

After a while her mouth relaxed and a little more blood ran out. Carefully he wiped it away and saw that she had stopped breathing. He continued to sit there, holding her; and when the Police came at last and found them, they took him without any trouble.

CHAPTER SIXTEEN

THE Police psychiatrist tapped with his pen on the surface of his desk. The small, hard noise of it was sterile in the silence of the office.

"Mr. Bruner," he said, "you're resisting me."

"Why shouldn't I?" demanded Kil.

The psychiatrist sighed and put down the pen and rubbed one hand wearily across his eyes. With his face relaxed, he looked younger than he had, a lean young man with hair receding sharply from the temples. He put his hand back on the desk and leaned forward again.

"We do what we have to," he murmured, almost to himself. "Mr. Bruner, were your physical relationships with your wife—"

"Go to hell!" said Kil.

The psychiatrist nodded slowly and relaxed back into his chair.

"Yes," he said. "Why not? This isn't the kind of job I'm supposed to do, anyhow." He got up briskly and suddenly, as if he had just come to a decision. "Wait here," he said and went out.

Kil waited. He had been in deadlock with the psychiatrist since the Police had brought him here to Headquarters, four hours ago. A little more time would make no difference.

The psychiatrist did not come back. What did come were two Policemen who escorted him to another office, a larger one this time. Inside, the psychiatrist waited for him; and another man, a heavy, balding man in advanced middle age with a thick, reddish complexion. Both men showed the bright eyes and flushed faces of anger. Both were standing and they turned on Kil as he entered.

"Get out," said the heavy man. The two Policemen left, closing the door behind them. "So you're Bruner."

"Yes," said Kil.

"This is Hagar Kai, Mr. Bruner," put in the psychiatrist, "present six-month head of the Police."

"I'll handle this!" said the Police head. "You don't seem to realize what you're up against, Bruner. We've just caught you red-handed in conspiracy and armed violation of the Peace. Do you know what that means? Do you?"

"No," replied Kil.

He looked at Hagar Kai. A strange thing was happening to him. Kai's anger, the unjustness of the accusation, above all, everything he had been through that day, now culminating in this, should by all the ingrained patterns of his nature have evoked his furious resentment. It had always been that way with him.

But now there was nothing. Kil's emotions lay still and cold. He saw through the rage and bluster of the Police head as through a clear pane of glass. The man was bluffing. What's more he was making himself look ridiculous in the process.

"No, I don't know," said Kil.

"Well, you'll find out."

"Suppose," Kil said. "You tell me what you want."

"Some straight answers, that's what we want!" Hagar Kai thumped the desk before him with his fist; and then, when Kil's expression did not change at this, let the hand drop limply at his side. "It's no use, Alben," he said, turning to the psychiatrist. "He doesn't want to help himself."

The psychiatrist said nothing. Hagar Kai turned back to Kil.

"I wouldn't bother with you if it wasn't for the fact your friend with the gun, and the hunchback, got away," he said, harshly. "As it is I'll give you one more chance to tell us. Where's McElroy?"

Even Kil's new self-control was not capable of taking this without staggering. He stared at Hagar Kai.

"McElroy?" he repeated.

The Police Head stared at him apoplectically.

"Don't you know?" said Kil, foolishly.

"Where is he?"

A small light of understanding began to illuminate the murky confusion in Kil's mind.

"So McElroy *is* the Commissioner, after all," he said. He shook his head at Hagar Kai. "How should I know where he is?"

Hagar Kai threw up both hands in a gesture of

exhausted patience and dropped heavily into a chair behind the desk.

"I still suggest," the psychiatrist said, "that you try explaining to him, first."

All right. All right!" Hagar Kai rested his arms on the desk and glared up at Kil. "Although he knows more about it than I do. Here it is, Bruner. We know you were working with McElroy—"

"What?"

"Now, don't bother to deny that. He put you on the payroll of his section when you came to see him about your wife. I say, we know you were working for him. He was engaged on a special case and thought you might help. Now—"

"What case?"

"You know as well as I do!" snarled Hagar Kai. Kil looked narrowly at him.

"Not—" he said, "the Project?"

"Damn it, Alben!" exploded the Police head, swinging around upon the psychiatrist. "I told you he knows all about everything!"

"If he doesn't, he's learning fast," retorted the psychiatrist, drily. "With your help."

Caught short, Hagar Kai checked himself and threw a startled glance at Kil. He turned back to the attack.

"What do you know about the Project?"

"I've heard about it," said Kil.

"And what else have you heard about?"

"Sub-E," said Kil, "the Societies, the O.T.L." He paused. "The Commissioner."

"There!" cried the Police head. "You admit knowing about McElroy."

"I don't know anything about McElroy!" retorted Kil. "I just happened to hear that he was known as the Commissioner. And while we're at it as a citizen I'd like to know why you, as the responsible man in the Police, have been letting someone else without legal authority take over part of your powers."

"The Police was set up in a way that kept its hands tied," replied Kai, harshly. "We're all held down to six months in one post, too. Besides there's the restriction that no one man can hold the post I'm in more than once in his lifetime. You can't run an organization under those conditions." He stopped suddenly, staring at Kil. "What do you mean *as a citizen*? You're under arrest. You haven't any citizenship rights."

"Now, hold on, Kai—" began the psychiatrist.

"Shut up, Alben. It's my responsibility and my authority. Well, Bruner, do you want to go on with this farce of pretending there's things I can tell you about this situation?"

"Please," said Kil, grimly.

"All right. I'll make it short and sweet. McElroy left his office here to work with you. All we got from him were messages, the last of which was to pick you up for a security check. You know the results of *that*. Now we've got information that the Societies are planning a revolution—and we've lost contact with McElroy. He doesn't check with us, and we've no way of locating him. Maybe, even, he's sold us out to the Societies. We won't know until we find him. And the quickest way to find him is have you tell us where he is."

"I tell you," said Kil, "I don't know. From that first day when I spoke to him here, I've never seen him again."

"You're a liar. But you're going to tell us the truth." Kai leaned forward and his eyes glittered. "The world is ready to blow up and if you think I'm going to let due process of law stand in my way at this late hour, you're badly mistaken. There're ways to get information out of men like you and here at Headquarters is as good a place as any to put them to use. You had your chance. Now I'll do it my way. I'm going to have you—"

"All right, Kai!" broke in the psychiatrist, suddenly. "That's enough. If you're planning anything like that for this man, you should've left me out of the room where I couldn't hear it. I can't let you do this."

Hagar Kai swung on the other like a cornered bull.

"Can't?"

"Won't." The psychiatrist's face was pale except for two spots of burning color on his lean cheeks. "If you're going to make this man disappear while you work information out of him, you're going to have to make me disappear, too— and I'll leave it up to you to take on the psychiatric Association when I don't show up at home for dinner tonight."

They locked eyes.

"Alben, you young fool," said Kai, hoarsely. "I knew your father. I've known you for thirty years. I—"

The psychiatrist said nothing. He stood immovable, his eyes unwavering and uncompromising.

The Police head slumped into his chair.

There was silence in the office. Finally, after a long minute, the man named Alben spoke.

"Sorry, Kai," he said. "But I think he's telling the truth. And even if he isn't—there's no exception to justice."

"Go on, get out of here, both of you," said Kai. "No, wait—" he raised his head and gazed burningly at Kil, "not you. If I can't go outside the law, I can at least give you all the law allows. Did you ever hear of Class Four?"

"Class Four?" echoed Kil. "*Unstab* Class Four?"

"Yes."

Kil shook his head. "No. There's only three classes, Stab, or Unstab."

"You're wrong," said the Police Head, in a heavy voice, "there's an Unstab Class Four. For active enemies, violators of Peace."

In spite of himself, Kil felt a queer shrinking inside him.

"How much?" he said. "How much time do you have in that?"

Hagar Kai looked at him.

"Twenty-four hours," he said. "Every twenty-four hours you move. Three hundred and sixty-five different locations every year. You'll sleep in a transient hotel every night. Your food, and drink and clothing, will be handouts from the Police, one day's supply at a time."

The words dropped on Kil's ear like stones, one by one, into a deep well.

"You can't do that!" cried Kil. "My wife—I've got to look for my wife—" he caught himself suddenly.

"Look where you like," said Hagar Kai, "as long as you never look for more than a day in any one place. And I wish you luck, Bruner." He sat leaning forward and watching Kil. Kil stood silent, seeing the man's purpose now and refusing to be drawn. The silence stretched out in the office.

Five minutes later, they put him out through one of the gates to Headquarters. Two Policemen had stripped the old Key from his wrist and escorted him there. Now, as he stood in the open street, they handed him a new Key and a meager roll of possessions, one change of clothing, some toilet articles and three small food packages.

"Put the Key on," ordered the younger of the two. He was a round-faced boy barely out of his teens, and this sort of thing was obviously new to him. He spoke with a gruffness and glare that did not succeed in covering up the embarrassment and a sort of horrified sympathy in him.

Automatically, Kil took the Key and roll. He stood looking at them for a moment in his hands, the couple of pounds of small things that were now his total estate and his life. For a long moment he looked at them; and then he handed them back to the young Policeman.

"No thanks," he said, gently. "I don't think I'll be wanting these after all."

And the world seemed to fall like a cloak from his shoulders, as he turned and went.

CHAPTER SEVENTEEN

On the third day after that, Dekko found him.

Kil had come to a halt finally a little back in the Cascade mountains, where they run into British Columbia, Canada. The aircab that had brought him out from Vancouver glittered a little foolishly on the rocky hillside in the thin, brilliant sun of early mountain morning, as if it could not quite reconcile itself to being so far from civilization. Kil sat apart from it, before a little fire of dry branches—for the morning was cool—staring unseeingly at the almost invisible flames.

Suddenly a speck in the air grew to a recognizable shape of another aircab and this came on, as an eagle sheered away suspiciously, to land on the slope beside Kil's vehicle. Kil looked up, but did not stir, as Dekko got out and came toward him.

The little hunchback stopped on the far side of the fire and looked down at him.

"Now, what did you do for that?" he said.

Kil smiled a little, opened his mouth as if to explain, then closed it again. He shrugged. It was too big. Perhaps the time would come finally when he could answer that question; but not now.

"Where've you been? I've been chasing you for two days now without being able to come up with you. What've you been doing?"

Doing? He had been traveling, in constant motion on rocket and mag ship, from Duluth, to Mexico City, Buenos Aires, Rio, Capetown, Timbuktu, Algiers, Madrid, Amsterdam, Oslo . . . the list ran on indefinitely. He had not been hungry—except for a little while on the first day. And he could not remember sleeping, although he must have dozed from time to time in his rocket or mag ship seat. Now, he was neither tired nor hungry, only withdrawn in a strange way, as if he had turned in on himself. People, he remembered, had mostly not noticed that he was Keyless. When they had, they had been shocked, horrified, fascinated. . . .

He shrugged again, in answer to Dekko's question.

"Listen, you don't have to give up!" The small man's voice was filled with an unusual, urgent concern. "We can fix it. I can fix it. You can go back and they'll have to give you your Key again. What if it is Class Four? Once you've got it, I can fix things up so you won't know it from Class A. There's nothing I can't get. You musn't give up."

That roused him.

"I'm not giving up," he said.

"I got food and something to drink in the cab. You got to eat. Clean up and shave. I got some clothes in there, too. If there's anything else you want, just ask me. I can get anything for you. Anything."

"I don't want anything," said Kil. "I just want to think. Go on back."

Dekko sat down obstinately opposite the fire.

"I'm not leaving until you come with me," he said.

"Then sit quiet," said Kil. He got to his feet and motioned Dekko down as the smaller man started to scramble up, also. "It's all right. I'm just going off a few feet. Sit still."

He walked away across the rubbled shelf of rock and sat down again at a distance of some twenty yards. The fresh breeze coming up the river gorge blew coolly around him, but he felt it as something remote and unimportant. He no longer needed the warmth of the fire. His mind, narrowing down now to the essentials of his search, was dispensing with irrelevancies.

He was remembering a great many things. He had reviewed in his mind the years he had lived with Ellen and what he looked for was almost, but not quite, there. He had moved among the world of people as a spectator, and looked at it; and what he wanted was almost, but not quite, there. He had seen, talked to, experienced, Stabs and Unstabs, Dekko, McElroy, Ace, the blond boy, Toy, Bolievsky, Mali, Melee, and an old botanical technician that loved his bug. And the answer was almost but not quite, there.

The answer, he realized, quite quietly and suddenly, was in himself.

He felt a long sigh of accomplishment slip through him. He lifted his eyes to the mountains, and to the eagle, circling slowly against the blue unclouded sky. And he let his mind, like the bird, go free.

He stood apart from himself and imagined himself looking down on his seated body, sitting on the mountainside, with Dekko and the fire a short distance away. And then he stepped his point of view away and up, so that he looked down at himself still, but from the edge of a clifftop several hundred feet above. He saw himself, with his mind's eyes, from the new viewpoint—small and motionless, with Dekko, small and motionless beside the fire, pale in the daylight.

Again, he stepped away, so that he hung in air above the level of the tallest peak and saw the mountainside upon which he sat, and a speck that was he, and Dekko and the fire together, so small that they could not be made out separately. Again he moved away; and the whole continent lay spread below him.

The sky was black above him, little patches of cloud were white and distant below, as they looked seen from an intercontinental rocket at the peak of its arc above the earth. One more stride upward into the blackness and the face of the Earth from Pole to Pole hung before him with the bright line of the dawn creeping westward across the ocean.

He stepped back and saw the stars.

He stood back from the Milky Way.

From the galaxy.

From the island universe.

From the total universe.

From . . .

And then he was through.

CHAPTER EIGHTEEN

Kil got up and walked across the rocky ledge to Dekko and the fire. The sun was westering toward the early mountain twilight, for a good part of the day had come and gone as Kil sat apart. The decaying light lay obliquely along the upper walls of the gorge and the lower walls were already in shadow. The fire burned ruddily and fitfully in the light air; and its bed was ringed with charred, unburnt half-ends of dry limbs, where it had been replenished many times. Dekko had fallen into a doze; and he sat cross-legged and hunched over, his hump pronounced and his sharp chin digging into his chest. Kil looked down on him, feeling a sympathy, almost a tenderness for the smaller man, not unmixed with a certain amusement.

Kil leaned over and shook one shoulder gently. Dekko woke at once, his head springing up.

"Oh—Kil—" he said. He shook his head as if to shake the last shreds of sleep from his brain. "What's up?"

"I am," said Kil. "I'm ready to go."

Dekko scrambled to his feet.

"Fine," he said. He shivered, rubbed his hands and held them to the fire. "Cold," he said. He took his hands away and energetically began to kick the burning embers apart, spreading them to die on the bare rock.

"Now—" he said.

"Now," said Kil, "I'm ready to take you up on your promise."

"Promise?"

"Didn't you say you could get me anything I wanted?"

"Yes—" Dekko stared curiously at him in the dimming light. "Just about anything, that is. What do you want?"

Kil smiled at him.

"Get me a submarine," he said.

Dekko stared at him.

"A submarine? A sub? You mean a submersible."

"No," Kil shook his head. "I mean a submarine. Something capable of going down a thousand feet or more."

Dekko continued to look at him for a long moment.

"You need some food and a good night's sleep," he said at last.

Kil said nothing.

"A submarine?"

"That's right."

"What for?" demanded Dekko.

"I know where Ellen is."

"Where?" asked Dekko sharply.

"I'll show you. Can you get the submarine?"

Dekko started to say something, checked himself, and ended briefly by saying, "I can try."

They took their aircabs back to Vancouver and Dekko buried himself in a call booth. After some little while he emerged, looking grimly at Kil.

"This is going to cost money, you know," he said.

"I suppose," said Kil.

Dekko, however, did not ask him for any. A deep-going craft had been located, it seemed, at one of the coastal geologic survey stations down the coast near San Luis-Obispo; off Pismo Beach, in fact. It could not be bought, rented or leased; but because of some intricately woven connections between Dekko and certain people on present duty at the station, it could be borrowed for a day or two.

"We'll have to move it overland," said Kil.

"That's all right," replied Dekko. "It's a ducted fan drive. Air on water—though it's going to be slow in the air." He stared at Kil with renewed curiosity. "Where are we taking it?"

"Later," said Kil. "Ask me that again, later."

He returned Dekko's gaze, calmly, and the little man, looking confused, dropped his eyes.

They took a magship down the coast and an aircab out to the station. It stood, bright-lit and empty-seeming, in about four fathoms of water far enough out from the beach so that the booming of the surf came with a curious faintness to their ears. The moon was overcast and hidden, and as Kil and Dekko stood at last on the walkway running around the inside of the enclosed dock, the unshielded glare of the lights made a wall of blackness out of its open door, night-empty to the sea.

"There she sits," said Dekko.

Kil looked down at the swelling, metal whale-back of the sub, moving imperceptibly as it floated in the dock, restrained by its magnetic tethering field. The little slap-slap of small waves against its side made short, impatient protest in the stillness.

Kil nodded.

"There's no one around here now, is there?" he asked.

"Not them," said Dekko. "Nobody wants to know anything about this. Why?"

"I just wondered," Kil looked at him, "are you sure you want to go along with me?"

Dekko blinked at him.

"Me?"

"Yes."

Dekko said nothing for a long minute, his eyes, bright and unrevealing as polished obsidian, on Kil.

"Kil," he said, at last. "You've been talking strange every since we left the mountains. You don't look out of your head, but—why wouldn't I want to go?"

"Because of what it means to you," answered Kil, softly, "because of what it means to me. Because if we go from here on together, we have to be honest with each other."

"I don't read you, Chief," said Dekko.

"Kil," said Kil. "Kil, not Chief, Dekko. And you do understand me. This is important to you. Is it important enough to be honest with me?"

"I'm always honest."

"With yourself, yes. Now, with me."

"I think you're fishing for something," he said.

"No." Kil shook his head. "I know. I just thought it would be easier for you if you came to it by yourself."

Dekko said nothing, only continued to match him with that bright, unwavering gaze.

"All right, then," said Kil, sadly, "take it off."

"Take what off?"

Kil sighed.

"The mask," he said.

Slowly the stiffness seemed to leak out of Dekko. He opened his mouth a little, then closed it again. Slowly his fingers came up under his chin as they had that day when, dressed as Uncle George, he had sat opposite Kil in the Unstab hotel room. The fingers hooked and pushed upward. And the face of Dekko crumpled and moved before them.

He spread his shoulders and straightened, slowly. Slowly, almost magically, his torso seemed to stretch and expand. The hump on his back bulged. There was a slight pop and it deflated all at once as the man stood up to his full height, short now, but no longer little, and no longer crippled-appearing as mask and hair came off together.

McElroy looked at Kil.

CHAPTER NINETEEN

Dawn was breaking again over the wide, ever-cold waters of Lake Superior when they reached it at last in their slow-flying craft. Indifferently, the white, clear light, too new for warmth, illuminated the slaty, rolling waves and the hills above the bouldered shore. McElroy, at the controls, sent the sub down through the yielding surface of the lake: down through the gray water, down through the green water, down through the black water. The great, tumbled blocks of stone scattered down the shallower slopes as if by some weird and silent, long-forgotten aquatic landslide, became more scattered and finally disappeared, leaving only a bare but rugged country of drowned ravines and hills, looking gray and palely startled in the centuries-forgotten light of the searchbeams from the fleeting sub. Who goes? Who breaks our ancient slumber, the wakened, silted hills seemed to cry, as with sound and glare the alien sub shot past and its distorting shadow flickered on oozy slopes and cliffs.

"Which way?" asked McElroy.

"To the right," said Kil, "about one o'clock."

McElroy altered direction slightly and sped on.

"Eight hundred feet," he said, reading the depth gauge. And a little later, "eleven hundred."

They had come at last to a level, wide and empty plain. Their searchbeams probed its featureless expanse for a hundred yards before them.

"Where?" asked McElroy.

"Keep going," said Kil.

They continued on over the monotony of the bottom plain. Here there was nothing to mark distance or direction, only the occasional outcropping of basalt, swelling up out of the silt like the flank of some gigantic, mudded hog. Only once, startlingly, across this sterile-seeming plain, there wandered into the searchbeam's funnel of illumination the unexpected apparition of a snouted ten-foot sturgeon, waving his forked tail in slow astonishment at encountering a traveler even larger than his own large self.

"How do you know where you're going?" asked McElroy.

"Partly feel—partly logic—" said Kil. He smiled a little. "That doesn't explain it very well, does it? Maybe somebody else can do a better job of it than I can."

"Do you know what we're looking for?"

"Yes," said Kil, slowly. "I don't know just what it'll look like—" he broke off suddenly, gazing out through the front observation window of the sub. "There, I think."

They had come at last upon a rising mound, all but identical with the basalt heaves, except for the fact that this was more circular, more regular and more vast. Silt covered this, too; but for one short minute they were treated to the impossible sight of a slim woman-figure, unprotected under all those vast tons of water except for ordinary kilt and tunic, who waved when she saw them and turned to the mound. Immediately an opening, large enough to admit the sub, yawned before them. She slipped through and disappeared, waving them on.

They followed her in to a vast lock which was drained of water with a sudden rush, leaving them foolishly stranded in a shallow basin. Kil went back through the sub with a rush; and when McElroy followed him in emerging from the hatch a moment after, he was already holding the girl tight to him, the girl that had waved them in through the lock. They stood as lost as lovers are, on the metal flooring of the lock, while the heavy air around them reeked of the flat and fishy smell of the lake bed—and noticed none of it.

After a little while, they let each other go a little, though they did not really step apart, and they both looked at McElroy.

"You wife, I suppose," said McElroy dryly.

"Yes," said Kil. "Ellen, this is—I don't know your first name."

"David," supplied McElroy.

"David McElroy, my wife Ellen."

"I know about him," said Ellen. Under the brilliance of the overhead sunbeams and in the damp air, her blonde hair and blue eyes alike seemed touched with little diamond highlights. "We all know about him. How are you, David?"

McElroy shrugged, as if the unaccustomed mantle of his first name sat uneasily upon him.

"No different than usual—Ellen," he answered. His voice sharpened. "Where's this Project Group of yours?"

"I'll take you to them, in a moment," said Ellen. "We're all here, waiting for you—and Kil." She glanced up at her tall husband. "Kil, why did you bring him?"

"Things have to come to a head," said Kil. He looked at her, suddenly softening. "Don't worry for me," he said, gently.

"But I don't know what they'll do." Her voice was abruptly a little pitiful. "Chase called them all in—from all over the world. We've never been all together like this before. We're just people, after all, like anyone else. We can make mistakes, too. Oh, Kil!"

"Who's Chase?" McElroy's voice cut hard across the conversation. Ellen turned to him.

"My great-grandfather, Bob—Robert Chase. He's the only one of us we call by the last name. He's—well, he's old; and he's Project Head." She looked up at Kil. "You've met him, darling. It was him, at Acapulco and—"

"In that Unstab hotel in Duluth. I know;" finished Kil, for her. "Are they waiting for us?"

"Yes. But I wanted to speak to you for a moment by myself, first. Kil—" her eyes were a little fearful, "you understand, we'll be together from now on. It'll be all right, whatever they decide."

Kil took his hands from her; and his face hardened a little.

"No," he said.

"But you're one of us now, Kil. You're part of the Project. You have to go along with what the majority decide."

He looked at her with eyes like agates.

"Which side are you on?" he demanded.

"Oh, yours, Kil! I'm with you!" In her agitation she caught his arm and clung to it, as if to deny any shadow of a barrier between them. "You know that." She even shook his arm a little, angrily. "It's what it may mean to you. It's just that they'll expect you not to fight them."

"Why?" he said, looking down at her.

"Because you're one of them, one of us."

"Am I?" he asked. His voice deepened; and he stared at her, unwaveringly. "What I am, I made myself. I broke my own prison. I threw away my Key, alone. I sat by myself on that mountain and what I found, I found myself, without their leave and without their help. I did what I did for you, and for me. I bought my freedom and I'm not going to trade it back again."

"But this hasn't anything to do with you! It's about the rest of the world."

"Isn't it my world! Aren't the people in it my people, as much as theirs?"

"No. No!" she clenched her hands together. "We have to work together that's all."

He looked at her with a strange light in his eyes.

"There's no *have to* any more," he said.

She looked up at him and shook her head slowly, pain on her face.

"Oh, Kil!"

"There's not even any *have to* between us, any more."

"Kil!" she cried. "Don't say that! Don't ever say that. I'm always with you, against them, against anyone, against everything!"

His face softened. He put his arm around her shoulders again; and she clung to him.

"I know," he said.

"You'll forgive me if I don't understand any of this," put in McElroy. Kil looked over at him.

"It's just that we've reached an end to force," he said. "You'll see." He looked down at Ellen. "I think we'd better go now."

Ellen let go of him and stepped back. She turned and led them across the wet and shining floor to a disk elevator set against one of the rising walls. They stepped together onto one disk and dropped downward.

They passed several levels, opening on the corridors of what seemed to be dwelling quarters, and finally stepped off before a small, but solid door, the only exit from the equally small hall or alcove in which they had alighted.

"The auditorium," said Ellen, nodding at the door. She went forward and opened it. The voice of the old man she had called Chase, speaking in measured accents, came through to their ears. Ellen beckoned; and Kil, with McElroy, came up and went through the door.

He found himself on the small, semi-circular floor of what looked like an overlarge lecture room. The flat side of the floor was backed up against a high wall, from which projected a small stage, perhaps six inches above the floor, on which stood a lectern and, behind it, Ellen's great-grandfather. Around the rest of the room rose steeply, tier on tier, an amphitheater of crowded seats, all filled by listening people.

CHAPTER TWENTY

THERE were, in that room, between three and four hundred people, ranging from the very young to the aged, though the young predominated. Meeting their combined gazes with a discernment that would have been entirely foreign to him a few weeks earlier, Kil was able to sort out perhaps six generations, of which those of Ellen's age were clearly in the majority. There was a curious openness about the faces of the younger ones that puzzled Kil with a sense of haunting familiarity, before he suddenly realized where he had seen something like it before. It was next-of-kin to the wide-eyed interest of very young children and animals, those who had not lived long enough in the world yet to make the acquaintance of Fear.

Chase, the old man, had stopped speaking as they entered; and he turned to look at them as well. His eyes picked out Ellen and Kil, swung to McElroy, and back to Kil again.

"Why did you bring this man?" he asked.

"Because I thought he ought to be here," said Kil.

"Why?"

"Because I've been trying to find you—" broke in McElroy, quickly. "There's an emergency—a matter of life and death for everyone in the world. I had to find you."

Chase's eyes glared at him for a moment, then softened.

"We all know you, David," he said gently. "By reputation, if nothing else. You're a good man; but—what can *we* do for you?"

McElroy came two swift steps forward toward the lectern. He spoke directly to the old man in a tense and eager voice.

"Listen—" he said. "I know why you were set up here. You were set up at the same time Files was set up; isn't that right? Files was only a temporary solution to the problem of keeping people from blowing themselves up. You were to find a permanent one; isn't that right?"

Chase stood looking down at him for a moment. A look of pain crept across his face. Finally, he nodded.

"Yes," he said.

"Well, now's the time," said McElroy. "Files is licked. The Police are licked. We're up against something now Files can't check. It's up to you."

Again the look of pain crossed Chase's face. Slowly he shook his head.

McElroy stared.

"No?" he cried, like a man who has just heard his own death warrant read aloud.

"David—" said the old man, with effort, "we haven't anything for you. You don't know—"

"I know you've had a hundred years!" said McElroy, furiously.

"David," said the old man again, "you don't understand. A hundred years ago we knew, here in our Project, that occasionally a rare individual was able to do things in apparent contravention of physical laws. Today, after all those years since they gathered us and isolated us here to work for a solution, we only know those same things are being done not in contravention, but *outside* the ordinary laws of physics."

"What do you mean?"

"It's—not easy to explain. When these things happen—when we make them happen—there's no transfer of energy. The causes and effects operate below the level of energy; that's why we call this Sub-E, Sub-Energy. We've discovered a new field of silence. We've found out that the physical laws can be merely the manifestations of a philosophy of the individual mind. Through the system of that philosophy the physical universe can be partially manipulated. But by each person only for himself. For example, *I* can walk through walls; but I couldn't take you by the hand and lead you through them. That's both the blessing and the curse on this Sub-E of ours, because on account of that aspect of it, it can't ever be used to hurt someone else—but by the same token, it can't be used to help them, either."

McElroy leaned forward, his face etched with passion.

"Then teach people how to use it for themselves!" he said.

"If we only could!" answered Chase. "If we only knew how! But that's just what we don't know. For those who already have the ability, we can do a lot. We can teach them and train them to large and complicated uses of their talent. But to kindle the fire of it in a cold mind—that's the thing we've never succeeded in doing, even with some of our own people in the Project that've been with us from the beginning. Rarely, an adult individual gets it—suddenly and without warning from nowhere, the way Kil—" he looked at Kil, "—did. Children always get it—they seem to accept it instinctively if they're raised as ours are, with adults who have it. But those already grown up can't—" he stopped and lifted his hands hopelessly.

"Can't? Why not? What does it take anyway?"

"It takes," Chase stumbled, "an act of will, of faith somehow. You've got to believe you can do what you want to do, without reservation. Children can believe that way because they build their world on faith. Adults—" again he stopped; and shook his head.

McElroy stayed planted before him.

"You must!" he said between clenched teeth. "You must—"

Chase shook his head.

"We can't," he answered. "David, do you think we want people to have this any less than you do? It's just that we haven't found the answer, where it lies. And all we can do is go on looking for it."

"But there's no more time—" McElroy broke

off, biting his lower lip. Chase looked intently at him.

"Why not?" he asked. "Why not more time?"

McElroy opened his mouth; then hesitated. He closed it again. Behind them the door through which Kil and he and Ellen had just entered swung open once more.

"Won't you tell them, then, Dave?" asked a new voice, from beyond it. "Then I'll have to."

All the eyes in the room swung about, to look. The door was ajar; and, as they watched, slowly and ponderously through the opening, entering one by one with due care not to touch each other, came two figures completely encased in glittering phase armor. Oxygen tanks hung from their backs, the voice of the one that spoke coming from a speaker chest-high on the smaller of the two, a slim and pleasant looking young man. Beside him, the larger, a gigantic man, held, in addition, the heavy, awkward shape of an oxygen-catalyst flame thrower, the one unstoppable weapon capable of cooking a man, even inside the armor. For all its brutal size and weight the big man held it casually in one hand. For the big man was Toy; and the smaller man was Mali.

Silence held the room. Fantastically, the audience was not disturbed or alarmed. The odd, fear-free faces of the seated people rested on Mali and Toy only with surprise and curiosity until Mali, who had been running his eye along the front row of seats, pointed to one old man.

"Try him," he said.

Toy swung the muzzle of his weapon up and pressed the trigger. Kil saw sudden fear leap into the eyes of the man and understood suddenly that this must be one of the original project members who had never achieved Sub-E. But, even as he tensed to jump forward, Ellen was quicker. In the same second, she had stepped in front of the old man. The white, spurting flame struck her, wrapped her, and flared ceilingward, holding her for one brief second in its roaring heat like some new, slender phoenix, fire-triumphant, burning yet unconsumed. Then Toy released the trigger, the flame and roaring vanished; and Mali chuckled in the sudden stillness.

"Just testing," he said, lightly. "You can throw that away now, Toy."

The giant tossed the thrower from him. It fell loudly and heavily on the polished dark floor of the amphitheater and rolled twice to a stop.

"Who're you?" demanded Chase. The old man's face was white with horror and anger.

"The one Dave didn't want to tell you about," Mali smiled at him. "My name's Mali, and I head the combined Societies. I followed Kil here." He nodded across the space that separated them. "Hello, Kil."

Kil looked grimly back at him.

"Melee's dead," he said, bluntly.

For a second, a thin film gauzed over Mali's eyes. They seemed to go blind and opaque, like the eyes of a man who turns inward to gaze at his own soul.

"Yes—on Tuesday, wasn't it?" he murmured. "I turned around for just a moment in the corridor—and she was gone—just last Tuesday—"

A shiver trembled him for a moment. Then his eyes cleared and he looked back at Kil and smiled.

"You've been a good guide," he said. "We

planted a small tracer set in the bone behind your
left ear during the Search. Didn't you feel anything there when you woke up? We've never been
far behind you since."

"I want to know what you're doing here,"
snapped Chase.

Mali looked at him.

"I've come to collect this last piece of my
world," he said.

"Collect your world?" Chase stared at him,
dumbfounded.

"My world," replied Mali. He looked at McElroy. "Eh, Dave?"

McElroy's eyes were ice behind which banked
fires burned.

"Yes," he said, expressionlessly.

"I don't understand you," said Chase.

"Do you see this?" asked Mali. He moved his
hand to his waist. The armoring field covering his
fingers flowed into the field about his body; and
the fingers closed on a small, tan box at his belt,
the thumb resting on a little button atop the box.
"If I push this down, it'll send out a signal that
will result in certain—mechanisms being put into
action at various points about the world. And
once that's done, you won't have to worry any
longer about the people who don't have Sub-E."

Chase stared at him, puzzled.

"This is nonsense," he said.

"No. Remember the Lucky War? Remember
what Files and the Police were set up to guard
against? Well, you waited too long to take over
from them. That's what Dave here was trying to
tell you. Whether the world lives or dies is up to
me."

Chase's wrinkled eyelids slowly drew up and back. His eyes opened and his face stiffened. Slowly, as if with great effort, he turned his head from Mali to look at McElroy.

"David," he said, "this can't be true—"

"Why not?" said McElroy, in a dead voice. "Why do you think I— the Police would admit we're licked? Why do you think he's so sure of himself?" He stood slightly spraddle-legged, shoulders hunched a little, head thrust forward, his gaze burning on Mali.

"But—" Chase turned back to Mali and his voice struggled. "You couldn't. It'd be wholesale murder—you wouldn't—"

"Why wouldn't he, Chase? Why wouldn't he?" said McElroy, his gaze still fixed on Mali. "They are CH bombs?"

"Of course," answered Mali. "Didn't you know?"

"Not in details," said McElroy.

Chase was staring at Mali in horror.

"What right have you got—to even think," he said, "of murdering four billion human beings?"

"As much right as the next man," retorted Mali, looking up at him abruptly. "What's four billion anyway, but a number? What's it to you? Tell me, are you four billion times as shocked as if I'd told you I was going to murder just one man?"

"You're a devil," said Chase hoarsely. "No— you're the devil!"

"I'm a man!" said Mali. He smiled a little and softened his voice. "Just like you, Chase."

"But the only ones who could come through something like that would be us—the ones with Sub-E! Would you want to kill yourself, too?"

"Of course not," answered Mali. "I'm safe for the moment here in my armor. It's just a matter of staying safe for a month or so afterward. And then, after the radiation's gone; and the wind's blowing the stink out of the dead cities—I can start the world over again in my own way with my own people that I've got tucked away in a safe place."

He looked up at the old man. The empty silence grew between them.

"So you see," said Mali, softly. "It is my world. I own it— and all of you. Or would you want to be the one to defy me and make me push this button?"

"It's too late, Mali," Kil said.

Mali looked at him quizzically, and smiled.

"Too late? Why, Kil?"

"Because I've found the answer these people have been seeking for a hundred years," he answered. "I know how to make it available to anyone—Sub-E."

The eyes of all the room were upon him.

CHAPTER TWENTY-ONE

There were two in the room that he must convince.

In the little suspension of time, the momentary breath-caught silence that followed the second of his announcements, it seemed to Kil that time gathered itself like a breaking wave, poised for a second above the frail craft, the *Santa Maria* of his discovery and conviction. The winds that thrust him forward were all of the spirit. The ocean that dragged him back was all man's centuries of stubbornness and slowness to believe. Mali was looking at him from the middle distance with an interest as cruel and sharp as a crouching cat's.

"What new fairy tale's this, Kil?" he asked in his soft voice.

"No fairy tale," he said. He turned to Chase. "The truth."

The old man stared at him as if stricken with a senile paralysis. His firm old face sagged a little, looking numb and grey.

"Kil—" he said shakily, "Kil—" gradually the shock seeped out of him and life flowed back. His face tightened up again, became stern and hard.

"Lying won't help us here," he said, harshly.

Kil saw through the harshness to the sudden fear of a wasted lifetime lying beneath it.

"You found it too, Chase," he said. "Many times. You just didn't recognize it, that's all."

"Kil—what is it?" demanded McElroy. His voice burst in on the conversation with sudden, staccato insistence.

Kil looked over at him for a moment.

"The children," he said. "That's the only way anyone can achieve Sub-E; the way the children do it."

"I don't see what you mean," said McElroy, shaking his head, "You—"

"I did it," said Kil. "I scrapped everything I believed and started over again, like a child, without any ideas of my own. I was willing to do that, to get Ellen back. I would've believed the moon was made of green cheese and the stars were pumpkins—" he looked down at her beside him "if that would've helped me find her again."

"Yes indeed—fairy tales," murmured Mali slumberously; but his eyes on Kil were anything but slumberous.

"No," replied Kil, again. "Faith. What Chase saw—the complete faith of a child—coupled with something he didn't see, the urge of a child, the want of a child, the complete necessity of a child to learn to do what its parents do. No one works harder in their life at anything than they do at growing up. Adults forget what it was like—when they came once, helpless strangers into an alien world of giants with unknown languages and customs."

"Faith," said McElroy, sharply. "And effort. That it?"

Kil looked at him without answering for a moment.

"Part of it," he said at last.

McElroy's eyes held him unyieldingly.

"What's the other part?" he demanded.

The room trembled on the question. Across the short distance that separated them, Kil was aware of Toy staring at him with a strange curiosity in his black eyes.

He turned a little away from those eyes.

"There's something new in the world today," he said. "A new time coming for us all—" a sadness thickened his voice as he said it; a sadness neither for the good nor the bad of the past, but the familiarity of it, the part of his life it had been. And he could see from the faces in the audience that his emotion had somehow got through to them, too; so that, without understanding, they felt the sorrow as well. Their quick empathy caught him up and drew him on, so that he went on to say more than he had intended. "Already, the old ways are dying. Soon they'll be dead and buried, in histories and monuments. And to the people in the new times they'll be unreal, we'll be unreal, like something out of a book, or old woven figures on a medieval tapestry." He looked aside at the bare and gleaming wall of the amphitheater, feeling with unfocused eyes out of the new depths in him, a vast inexpressible, irrational sorrow, like the remembered sound of violins in the twilight winding the lost chords of memory around his throat to choke him into silence.

Ellen reached out and put her hand on his forearm; and the human touch of her brought him back to his purpose. He looked again at the people in the room, thrusting the thought of Toy from him.

"A new time," he said, crisply. "A new era— and Sub-E's only a by-product of it. It's the whole of which Sub-E is a part. The complete maturity of the individual, with everything that implies. The ultimate power, in Sub-E, for the individual to protect himself against anything but himself. And the ultimate sense of responsibility in a fully developed emphatic nature, to hold back from hurting others."

Mali laughed, almost relievedly.

"And this is what the John Q. Citizens of our time are on the verge of? Kil!" He shook his head and laughed again.

"But you don't tell us how; how to get it!" said McElroy, violently.

Slowly Kil turned to him. The shorter man's face was forged into a mask of intent and determination. Now was the time.

"For every person, it's different," said Kil. "Everyone has to find it for himself by facing up to the weaknesses in himself and strengthening them. My weakness was that I didn't want to concern myself about the world. I wanted it to trundle along by itself and not bother me; and I was set to do just that until—" he glanced at Ellen, "I found there was something I wanted more."

"And mine?" asked McElroy.

"Don't you know?" said Kil.

McElroy frowned, the sharp effort of his con-

centration cutting deep the short line between his
eyebrows.

"No—" he said, "no—"

Mentally, Kil crossed his finger.

"Think, Dave," he said, gently. "Chance
brought you into the world more intelligent than
most people. Impatience with their slower minds
drove you from them. But loneliness drove you
back. And your full conscience blocked the self-
ish path for you, that Mali's taken to personal
power. So you took it on yourself to work for and
protect people. That way your conscience and
loneliness were both satisfied. But if the day
comes at last when you're not needed any longer,
then you'll have to face yourself all over again,
won't you? You'll have to find a new purpose, a
purpose—"

He let his voice die, for something was happening to the other man. For a long moment, as Kil
spoke, there had been no change. And then abruptly, the spark of awareness in McElroy's eyes
seemed to go back, to dwindle and recede, back
and back until it appeared to have gone off into
some great personal infinity, on a pilgrimage from
which there would be no finding its way back,
except by the light of the lamp it searched for. For
a long, remembered moment, an empty man stood
before them all; and then, slowly, McElroy came
back once more to look again out of his own eyes.

"Yes," he said; and sighed—a sigh that had
some of Kil's earlier sorrow in it. Then, like a
tired, but satisfied man he straightened up and
smiled at them, a queer, sad, impish smile that
had something of the lost Dekko in it. And he held
out his hand, cupped, toward the audience.

"Sub-E," he said; and abruptly—in one fractionary moment, one infinitesimally brief bit of time—there sparked in his palm a tiny bit of fiery matter that was bright and hot as only a part of the sun could be; and then was gone again.

And so, the first one was convinced.

A long, pent-up breath soughed out through the room.

"Oh, God—" said Chase, shakily.

"Amen," said McElroy, lifting his face to the old man.

But Mali looked across the room to Kil and chuckled.

"And now you'll convert me, Kil?" he asked.

Kil slowly shook his head.

"I'd give a great deal to," he said. "You've got the guts, and the intelligence. If you'd face the fact that you're emphatically blind, open up that tight ego of yours—"

Mali laughed out loud.

"And give up the world, no doubt," he said, "for a little extra insight? No thanks, Kil. I'm not that much of a fool, to make that bad a bargain."

"Yes," said Kil, sadly. "I didn't think you would. You belong to the old days, Mali, the days that're already dead, when selfishness was a survival factor. It's twisted you so badly that you couldn't even love the one person in the world it was possible for you to love: your sister. You could only dominate her, warp her natural need for affection into nymphomania—and be the cause of her death."

For a second, Mali's face became a white and perfectly sculptured death-mask with rage. Beside him, Toy turned his head to look suddenly at

the smaller man, searching Mali's rigid features
with an abrupt, demanding interest, like a dog,
tense by a fox's hole, who suddenly thinks he sees
the blackness stir inside. But then, slowly, Mali's
face relaxed and the color came back. He smiled
again.

"Sticks and stones," he said, lightly. "No, you
won't convert me, Kil. Or anyone else."

"Yes we will," replied Kil, quietly. "We'll go
out from here, now; all of us in the Project, one by
one or two by two together, and talk to people in
the world as I've talked here. We'll show them the
way to search themselves for the road to personal
maturity;" he paused, then added, "and Sub-E."

Mali stared at him.

"You think I'd let you do that?" he said. "Make
one move, Kil, in that direction, and I press my
button. And what can you do about that?"

"I can't do anything," said Kil.

Mali smiled, a grim statue's smile.

"But," said Kil, "there'll be someone—"

Mali stiffened.

"Who?"

Kil turned away. *Murderer!* his mind shrieked
soundlessly at him. *Murderer!* He clamped his
jaw tight against the sickness in his heart and
spoke.

"There'll be a man," he said. "There'll be a man
somewhere who's come to see you clearly at last
for what you are, and what you're doing to the
world and him. A man of dreams—" Kil's back
was almost to Mali now. He spoke to the audience,
but without seeing them, "a man of frustrated
dreams, who's hunted his destiny for years, just
wanting the one opportunity, the one chance to

fulfill them. And now, when his eyes are cleared, he'll see at last the chance of it; the chance of making himself at last what he's lived to be and never been. And then he'll stop you, Mali."

Behind Kil, Mali's voice cut sibilantly across the silence.

"Are you a complete fool, Kil?" he said. "To dream of martyrs? And how can a martyr stop me?"

"I don't know," answered Kil, without turning. "I don't know. But when an idea becomes greater than a man; and a man is great enough to see that the idea is greater than himself, then there's nothing to stop him; not personal extinction or anything else. Because when you finally come to it, there's no point in living unless you have something to live for. The years of a lifetime are brief, after all. A man can fritter them away, or miser them up, or sometimes if he wants he can spend them all, all at once and together in one great purchase—" Kil looked out at the audience, "of a dream."

Behind him, Mali laughed loudly.

"Dream!" he said. "And dreamers!" Kil turned about to face him; and he went on. "Dreamers, Kil, are psychotics, people with poor, twisted, unnormal minds. I take good care they don't come too close to me."

"Are you sure?" said Kil. "How can you tell about men with dreams, Mali? You've never had any. So how can you say what this dream of his can mean to one man who carries the hope of the race in his hands, when he sees this moment of his, this short, soon-lost moment of his come up? How can you tell what will happen then?"

Toy took a sudden, ponderous half-step forward and Mali, without looking, gestured him back. Mali's eyes were still on Kil and they glittered feverishly.

"How can I tell?" he echoed. "Because I know what dreams are made of. They're made of air, less than air, of nothing. Only that."

"Only that?" asked Kil. "When they're inside a man?"

Mali laughed again, and his laughter rattled wildly about the walls. He threw his arms wide, leaving the box at his waist open and unhidden, except by the impenetrability of his armor.

"Attack me, then!" he cried. "You're the dreamer, Kil. Draw first, hero, and stop me; stop me now before I reach down and send this world you want so badly, to hell! Attack me! Conquer me! Conquer me with your dreams!"

In that second, while the world waited, Kil turned at last, meeting the eyes of Toy who stood like some great bulldog-man, pillar-legged beside Mali. The shielded candle-flame of hope within Kil leaped out, caught and flared up afresh on the answer in those black eyes. Across the short space their gazes met in final, open understanding; heart bared to heart, the chalice and the sword.

And so the second one was convinced.

So in that same moment it was accomplished, what Kil had set out to do; and the giant swung about and stooped. Like a mother lightly snatching up her child, Toy caught Mali to his breast. His great arms locked beneath the outflung arms of Mali, hugging the smaller man to him, holding the slippery, intangible surface of Mali's body armor fast against the slipperiness of his own,

locking the box and button away behind walls of
muscle, from the frantically scrambling fingers.

And both men's armor flared—into white and
fiery violence. Arcing on contact, forced and held
together by the enormous strength of Toy, the
equal and opposed fields flashed into violent
electronic flame, shooting out in all directions so
that an eye-searing nimbus of sparks coruscated
from the clasping figures.

Locked together, they stood, two men straining
in unheard struggle, motionless as statuary in a
furnace, cooking in their armor. Now black smoke
rolled upward on the tips of red flame as the
overloaded insulation of the body circuits went,
mixing in with the pale brilliance of the magnetic
aurora. Silent in the roaring midst, body to body,
face to face, slayer and slain swayed in a deadly
embrace. For a fractionary moment in the second
of their dying, Toy's face showed clear of the
ruddy smoke, his great head flung back, his eyes
closed, his face white offering to the god of his
purpose. There was a calmness on his features, a
look of peace, like that of someone who wins at
last to his heart's desire. And then the burning
insulation parted, the inner shields touched and
coalesced in a sudden, flaring explosion of incon-
ceivable heat that burnt them both like paper dolls
and left the auditorium drifting with white
smoke.

"This was fate," croaked Chase, "on our side.
This was fate or great luck. This was—" his voice
died as Kil's eyes raised to look at him. Kil's face
was ravaged with pain and sorrow and his voice
came emptily from the flat wasteland beyond all
cries and whimpers.

"This was this," said Kil, with his fingers still on the carbonized shoulder before him, white with life against its blackness, "This was Toy. He was a man."

EPILOGUE

THE warm air of the mountain meadow rocked in the drowsy heat of a June afternoon, and the weathered driver of the all-purpose bug, emerging from the hillside's small belt of pines into sunlight and the sound of shrilling crickets, stopped in surprise beside the young man and woman standing there. He thumbed aside the window and looked out.

"Hey!" he said.

"Give us a ride?" asked the girl.

"Sure." He stared hard at the craggy face of the tall young man, his own brown visage deepening into sharper lines and wrinkles with the effort of memory. His eyes, burned blue by the sun, considered them as he rolled the door of the bug open. "Don't I know you?" he asked as they climbed up into the seat beside him.

"You gave me a ride to Duluth once," answered the young man, closing the door. "I'm Kil Bruner. This is my wife, Ellen."

"Pleased to meet you," said the old man, looking at the aquamarine eyes and blonde hair of the girl between them. "Sure, I remember now." He geared the bug and they started forward with a jerk. "What're you two kids doing way up here?"

"Talking to people," said Kil. He held up one tanned, bare wrist for the old man to see. "About their Keys. . . ."

Gordon R. Dickson

MORE TRADE SCIENCE FICTION

Ace Books is proud to publish these latest works by major SF authors in deluxe large format collectors' editions. Many are illustrated by top artists such as Alicia Austin, Esteban Maroto and Fernando.

Robert A. Heinlein	Expanded Universe	21883	$8.95
Frederik Pohl	Science Fiction: Studies in Film (illustrated)	75437	$6.95
Frank Herbert	Direct Descent (illustrated)	14897	$6.95
Harry G. Stine	The Space Enterprise (illustrated)	77742	$6.95
Ursula K. LeGuin and Virginia Kidd	Interfaces	37092	$5.95
Marion Zimmer Bradley	Survey Ship (illustrated)	79110	$6.95
Hal Clement	The Nitrogen Fix	58116	$6.95
Andre Norton	Voorloper	86609	$6.95
Orson Scott Card	Dragons of Light (illustrated)	16660	$7.95

ANDRE NORTON

Witch World Series

Enter the Witch World for a feast of adventure and enchantment, magic and sorcery.

89705	**Witch World**	$1.95
87875	**Web of the Witch World**	$1.95
80805	**Three Against the Witch World**	$1.95
87323	**Warlock of the Witch World**	$1.95
77555	**Sorceress of the Witch World**	$1.95
94254	**Year of the Unicorn**	$1.95
82356	**Trey of Swords**	$1.95
95490	**Zarsthor's Bane** (illustrated)	$1.95

ANDRE NORTON

"Nobody can top Miss Norton when it comes to swashbuckling science fiction adventure stories." —*St. Louis Globe-Democrat*

07897	**Breed to Come**	$1.95
14236	**The Defiant Agents**	$1.95
22376	**The Eye of the Monster**	$1.95
24621	**Forerunner Foray**	$2.25
66835	**Plague Ship**	$1.95
78194	**Star Hunter/Voodoo Planet**	$1.95
81253	**The Time Traders**	$1.95

Kil stole a glance at Ellen. Her eyes were closed, her face tilted back a little and held still as if against some arrowing inner pain. She seemed to hold her breath. Watching, Kil felt the sudden explosion of instinctive alarm bells within him.

"Ellen!" he cried.

He started to reach out for her. And the world stopped.

On top of the cliff the diver checked suddenly, leaning out at an impossible angle over emptiness. The sea became rippled glass, with a whale spout hanging tiny and half-finished on the horizon.

Locked in stillness like everything else, Kil strained to turn his head, to move in any way, but could not. And then, from somewhere among the shadows on the terrace, there was movement . . . an old man dressed simply in kilt and tunic.

He came up to the table where Kil and Ellen sat.

"Now, Ellen," he said. It was a deep, tired voice.

Behind him, Kil heard the soft whisper of her skirt as Ellen rose. She came around the table slowly and stood looking down for a long moment into Kil's eyes.

"Ellen," repeated the old man. "Ellen. Come now."

There was no doubt about the tears in her eyes now. She bent swiftly and kissed Kil on his immobile lips. Then she turned, and the old man led her away, out of sight.

For Kil Bruner, the Known World Ends Here.

Books by Gordon R. Dickson:

ALIEN ART
ARCTURUS LANDING
PRO
SPACIAL DELIVERY
HOME FROM THE SHORE
THE SPACE SWIMMERS
ON THE RUN

From ACE Science Fiction

SF